All thoughts vanished as Cassandra Taylor met his gaze.

There was something new about her. But the curves, the dark hair falling over her shoulder, were all too familiar and brought memories rushing back... memories that should've been left in the past.

"Cassandra."

The door to the bar slid closed behind her. "I appreciate you seeing me without notice."

She took a step in and then another until she stood just on the other side of his desk. He could reach out and touch her, could see those navy flecks in her deep blue eyes.

He'd only had about a two-minute heads-up, but he certainly hadn't expected this onslaught of emotions to come flooding to the forefront.

"Luke."

Oh, hell. His name sliding through her lips had him recalling starry nights and heated moments. Agreeing to see Cassandra Taylor had been a huge mistake.

* * *

Fake Engagement, Nashville Style by Jules Bennett is part of the Dynasties: Beaumont Bay series.

In remembrance of Mistie, who always had a love for writing and hoped to have her work published one day. Our book chats and your infectious laugh are truly missed.

DESIRE

Recycling programs for this product may not exist in your area.

ISBN-13: 978-1-335-23296-0

Fake Engagement, Nashville Style

Copyright © 2021 by Jules Bennett

This edition published by arrangement with Harlequin Books S.A.

For questions and comments about the quality of this book, please contact us at CustomerService@Harlequin.com.

Harlequin Enterprises ULC
22 Adelaide St. West, 40th Floor
Toronto, Ontario M5H 4E3, Canada
www.Harlequin.com

Printed in U.S.A.

JULES BENNETT

FAKE ENGAGEMENT, NASHVILLE STYLE

USA TODAY bestselling author **Jules Bennett** has published over sixty books and never tires of writing happy endings. Writing strong heroines and alpha heroes is Jules's favorite way to spend her workdays. Jules hosts weekly contests on her Facebook fan page and loves chatting with readers on Twitter, Facebook and via email through her website. Stay up-to-date by signing up for her newsletter at julesbennett.com.

Books by Jules Bennett

Harlequin Desire

The Rancher's Heirs

Twin Secrets
Claimed by the Rancher
Taming the Texan
A Texan for Christmas

Lockwood Lightning

An Unexpected Scandal
Scandalous Reunion
Scandalous Engagement

Dynasties: Beaumont Bay

Twin Games in Music City
Fake Engagement, Nashville Style

Visit her Author Profile page at Harlequin.com, or julesbennett.com, for more titles.

You can also find Jules Bennett on Facebook, along with other Harlequin Desire authors, at Facebook.com/harlequindesireauthors!

One

"You've got another visitor."

Luke glanced up from his computer at the desk where he'd been hiding for most of the evening. "Tell her I'm busy," Luke told his bodyguard.

Normally he loved being out with his customers at his rooftop bar, The Cheshire, but not since that damn magazine article had thrust him into the spotlight.

Meet Luke Sutherland: Tennessee's Most Eligible Bachelor

That term, along with a photo of him in a pair of jeans with his dress shirt completely unbuttoned, had attracted every woman in the state—and some men, too—like some type of magnet.

Jake stepped farther into the room. "Uh, sir. It's Cassandra Taylor."

Cassandra Taylor?

That was a name he hadn't heard in years, but one he'd certainly thought of often enough.

All of that long black hair that he used to glide through his fingers and over his body. Her sweet smile that turned him on before she could even say a word. And the way he'd confided in her... He'd loved her once—she'd been his best friend.

Unfortunately, marriage hadn't been in the cards for him, not even to his best friend. Their paths had been destined for different directions and he'd let her go.

It had been the right choice.

So what was she doing back now after all this time? Surely she hadn't seen the article and now thought they had another chance at being together? That shot had been ruined when she'd left town nearly eight years ago with barely a goodbye. Oh, his brothers had blamed him at the time, and perhaps a portion of the blame did fall on his shoulders—he hadn't gone after her. But she hadn't stuck around to see if things could be worked out, either.

They'd both let go, and there was no going back after that.

"Tell her I'm busy, then," he repeated, almost wishing the uninvited guest had been a stranger.

Jake, his bodyguard and a top bouncer who had been with Luke since the opening of his first bar, knew full well the impact Cassandra had had on Luke's life. Luke continued to stare across his desk, but Jake didn't move.

"Is there a problem?" Luke asked.

"Let her in. She came a long way after all this time."

Luke leaned back in his leather chair and rested his elbows on the chair's arms. "When did you take her side?"

Jake laughed. "Her side? Sir, it's been years and I think you know where my loyalties lie, but you two have a history. She's not like those other women who have seen the article and are vying for the role of Mrs. Luke Sutherland. I doubt Cassandra is looking for a ring on her finger from you."

Luke swallowed. Maybe she wasn't, but he'd been prepared to put that ring on her finger when she left. Well, in theory. He'd had the ring, but somehow he'd never found the right moment to propose. And then she was gone. His brothers had ridiculed him—hell, he'd blasted himself on more than one occasion—but she hadn't even given him a chance to tell his side or explain his motives. Obviously, a marriage between them would have been doomed from the start.

If she'd been able to walk away so easily, then it was best he had never proposed. He'd been hurt, he'd been angry—maybe a part of him still was— but he wasn't the same naive guy he'd once been. Now he was glad he hadn't settled down. He loved the life he'd created and venturing back to his past wouldn't do anyone any good.

"Stop thinking so hard," Jake growled. "You know if you turn her away you're only going to be wracking your brain over what she might have wanted."

Damn it. Jake was right. That didn't make the fact that she was back any easier to digest. Apparently, she could still get to him after all this time. Or, maybe if he saw her, perhaps she wouldn't have any effect on him. She'd likely changed just as much as he had over such a long stretch of time.

There was only one way to find out.

Luke sat up and rested his arms on his desk. The decision volleyed back and forth in his mind. He had no clue what to expect. He hadn't seen Cassandra in years, save for the time he'd looked her up on social media a couple of years ago. He'd found her still single and still just as sexy as ever.

But his curiosity got the better of him.

With a deep sigh and some serious concerns, Luke nodded. "Fine. Bring her in."

As Jake left the office, Luke wondered what the hell he'd just done. Why would he purposely agree to see her again? They'd parted ways and agreed that was it. Yet now she was back. He didn't know why, but he had to assume her abrupt reappearance had to do with *Country Beat*'s article on him.

He'd been doing just fine with his bars in Beaumont Bay and Nashville. He'd been contemplating expanding to other cities. Maybe Chicago or Atlanta. He wasn't sure, but his life was always in forward motion. The only time he'd ever considered slowing down had been when he was with Cassandra, and look how that had turned out. Now, having any woman in his life would only hinder his career. He loved the country-music industry, loved the bar-and-restaurant lifestyle and loved combining the two. He didn't want to change any of it, not for anyone.

Luke got to his feet, then cursed himself. Should he be standing, as if he was anticipating her arrival? Or should he sit and try to appear relaxed? Sitting might be a jerk move, but he wanted her to know he wasn't affected by this visit. He could be casual with her, just like he would be with any other visitor.

Hell. She hadn't even gotten through the door yet and he was already tied up in knots. How would he feel coming face-to-face with her? A chunk of time had settled between them and the weight of that firmly took root in his chest. There was a heaviness he couldn't explain, but he didn't have time to try to.

All thoughts vanished as Cassandra Taylor stepped into the opening of his office and met his gaze. Luke realized he should've remained seated because she nearly knocked the breath out of him.

There was something so familiar about her, and yet so new. That confidence, with the straight shoulders, the tipped chin and the determined eye contact, was certainly new. But the curves, the dark hair falling over her shoulders and the slight smirk on her lips brought memories rushing back.

Despite her familiar beauty and new confidence, she was still the one who'd walked away and Luke had no desire to revisit the past. So he shoved away those emotions and memories. He'd gotten this far by living in the moment and taking control of his own destiny. Nobody and nothing would ever change that again.

"Cassandra."

The door to the bar slid shut behind her and she jerked around to see that she'd been closed in.

"An automatic door. That's fancy," she muttered as she turned back to face him. "I appreciate you seeing me without notice."

She took a step inside and then another until she stood just on the other side of his desk. He could reach out and touch her. He could see those navy flecks in her deep blue eyes.

He'd only had a two-minute heads-up, but he certainly hadn't expected this onslaught of emotions to come flooding to the forefront of his mind…and his body.

"Luke."

Oh, damn. His name sliding through her lips had him recalling starry nights and heated moments. No matter why she was here, he'd get her in and out. No way could he get caught up in her like he had in the past. He was perfectly fine remaining single… Wait. Was that why she was here? She'd seen that article and now she wanted to come back and secure her original role as his woman?

No way. That was a hard no.

Agreeing to see Cassandra Taylor had been a mistake. Somehow, he knew this moment would no doubt change his life forever.

Nerves curled into spirals in Cassandra's belly. She'd given herself a pep talk the entire drive here—all three hours. Luke was just a man and she was just a woman. There was no reason she couldn't approach him about her critical need. They were different people now.

When she'd left their relationship years ago, she'd done so because she'd had to guard her heart. Staying would only have caused more pain. Luke had been so set on moving ahead in his career and seemed perfectly content keeping her tucked in a corner, always assuming she'd be content to stay there. While she'd been proud of all he'd accomplished, she'd also wanted to be by his side. She'd wanted them to grow together…and she'd learned too late that they'd had two different visions of what they'd wanted out of life.

So she'd walked away, made a successful career for herself and absolutely loved the life she'd created in Lexington, Kentucky.

So why the hell was she so shaky now that she was back?

When Luke's intense stare became too much, Cassandra pulled together all her courage and forced herself not to turn and walk out. She stood her ground.

Clearly, he wasn't going to say anything, even though she'd called him by name to snap him out of whatever trance that had overtaken him. Although, he was likely waiting on her to explain why she'd shown up, out of the blue, after not a word in eight years.

"Your bar is amazing and Jake seems…intimidating," she began, not wanting to jump right into the real topic. "You've done really well for yourself."

"Jake does his job skillfully." Luke shifted his stance and rested his hands on his narrow hips. "But did you come all the way here to tell me what I already know?"

Okay, well, obviously his ego was still intact and he wasn't in the mood for the small talk she had rehearsed to lead up to her real reason for coming back.

Pulling in a deep breath, Cassandra jumped right in.

"No," she replied. "I came here to tell you I need a favor."

Luke stared another moment before that rich, familiar laugh filled the spacious office. Unable to stand still, Cassandra moved around and glanced at the black-and-white images on the walls. Pictures of Luke and his brothers. The Sutherland men were all handsome and powerful, and she had loved each of them like family...but none like Luke. Gavin, Cash, and Will had all been like her own brothers. She'd missed them when she'd left town without looking back.

But Luke... He'd left her bitter and angry. He'd strung her along, allowing her to think they'd spend their lives together, when he only cared about the next bar he could open or how quickly he could book the next big star so he could have bragging rights.

So she'd left.

Cassandra had gathered up the pieces of her shattered heart and continued on with her own dreams. She'd gotten along just fine in her career as a wedding coordinator, despite being jealous with each "I do" she helped create. And now that she'd branched out and opened her own company, she needed something amazing to make her stand out in a saturated industry. She needed a celebrity wedding.

And that's where the favor she was after came in. That's why she'd set aside her pride, and her carefully repaired heart, and driven the three hours to Beaumont Bay to put herself in front of Luke.

"I know Will is getting married." Cassandra turned from the images to face Luke once again. He still hadn't moved, but those eyes remained on her. "That's what I'm here about."

"Sorry, darlin', but he's already got a bride."

Cassandra sighed. "Obviously. I'm aware his bride is Hannah Banks. I want to be their wedding coordinator and you're going to get that job for me."

Silence settled between them and her heart pounded so loud, she could hear the rhythmic thump in her ears.

"You came all the way here to make that demand?" Luke circled the desk to stand right in front of her. "You could have called."

Oh, mercy. He smelled too damn good and seemed broader, stronger, sexier than ever. Maybe a phone call would have been better.

No matter. She was immune to his charms now. She'd known when she'd decided to ask for this

favor that Luke would be handsome and successful. He'd been both of those things when she'd
left. The hurt he'd left her with had trumped any
physical attraction.

"Would you have taken my call?" she asked.

Luke shrugged. "Sure, why not? We've both
moved on."

His eyes dropped to her lips and that flair of
arousal shot up again. She'd only been in the office for all of two minutes and already she wanted
him. Maybe it was the memories creeping up. She
had to keep reminding herself to stay in the present and focus on the real reason for her visit back
to the Bay. Luke owed her for the years she'd spent
with him, when she'd waited on him to commit,
and all the hurt he'd caused in the end. Cassandra
was ready to cash in his debt.

And yet, who could blame her for getting sidetracked by Luke Sutherland? Even if they hadn't
had an intimate past, the man would have demanded attention, with his dark gaze, his strong
jawline, and those broad shoulders. When he
crossed his arms and widened his stance, Cassandra swallowed the lump of arousal in her throat.

The man knew exactly what he was doing to
her. How dare he stand there and look so, so...

Ugh. Frustration was taking hold of her.

A shrink would have a field day in her head,
considering her past heartbreak when it came to

a man who'd refused to marry her, along with her current line of work helping happy couples walk down the aisle. Maybe she was just a hopeless romantic who still believed in the miracle of happy endings.

Just because things hadn't worked out for her didn't mean she didn't believe in love. She saw the reality of it every day as a wedding coordinator. Maybe one day she would find the man she was meant to be with.

Once upon a time, she'd thought for sure that man was Luke. Now she was glad she hadn't hung around any longer waiting for him. She'd seen that *Country Beat* article. Apparently, he still wasn't in the market for a wife.

"What makes you think I have any pull with Hannah?" he asked, jerking her attention to his low, gravelly tone. "She's a superstar. She's got her own entourage of people. I'm sure she has found her own wedding coordinator since they want to do something quick and small."

Cassandra smiled. "Do you think I would have come all this way if I hadn't done my research? She has no coordinator as of yesterday, which is why you need to get on the phone now and make an appointment with her for me."

The muscles in Luke's jaw clenched as he continued to stare at her. Cassandra really didn't want to pull the past into this moment, but she would do it if she needed to. She wasn't leaving this office without an appointment.

"What makes you think you'll get the job?" he asked.

"You get me the in-person meeting and I'll get the job."

Luke rested his hip on the edge of his desk and seemed to study her…and he also seemed to be considering her idea.

"Why is this job so important for you?" he asked.

"I started my own company," she told him. "It's only six months old. I worked for Brides and Belles for almost eight years and it was time to go out on my own. I need a celebrity wedding to push my business and put my name at the top of other celebrity lists."

Even if that meant swallowing her pride and begging.

Again, Luke landed that intense stare on her and she forced herself to remain calm and not fidget. He *had* to agree to this. He absolutely had to. Launching her own service, Be My Guest, had taken most of her savings and every ounce of her courage. She would fight with everything in her being to make this next career move a huge success…even if that meant putting her heart and sanity on the line once again and facing Luke Sutherland.

"I'll help you."

Cassandra nearly threw her arms around him, but then remembered touching him would be a terrible idea. Still, she couldn't stop the smile from spreading across her face.

She'd always believed in love, always wanted to see other couples be happy and help them create the most perfect day. She'd even envisioned her own perfect day with Luke way back when. But now...well, now she wouldn't allow herself to even mentally walk down the aisle—not until she found a man worthy of her. Now, all her energy was on making Be My Guest a success. And Luke was helping her do it.

"Luke, you don't even—"

"On one condition," he added, straightening and leveling his gaze on her.

Her excitement was short-lived as she heard his stern tone. "A condition?"

"You will help me in return."

He circled around the other side of the desk and pulled a magazine from a drawer. He slapped the magazine on the desktop, the harsh sound echoing throughout the office, and angled the article for her to see.

"That is ruining my life." He pointed to the open pages. "I'll get you that appointment if you pretend to be my very doting, very public fiancée until Will's wedding is over."

Cassandra waited for the punch line of this sick

joke. She'd waited so long for him to ask her to marry him. He'd been working toward opening his first bar, and she'd been trying to break in to planning weddings. But the longer she'd waited, the more he'd become involved in his work. One bar turned into another and he'd reached a point where he'd been too busy for her. Between bar openings, hiring of employees, and finding bands and artists to keep the stages full and the customers coming back, a solid wedge had formed between them. And, one day, Cassandra had realized she would never be able to compete for his affection.

The realization had stung because she'd supported him, had wanted him to fulfill his dreams as she chased her own. Unfortunately, he chased them so far, he forgot to take her along.

And now he was asking her to fake the one thing he'd never been willing to give her?

"You're not serious," she finally said, anger bubbling deep within her.

His stern face and steady stare told her he was quite serious. Now she just had to think about how badly she wanted this job. Planning a celebrity wedding would be invaluable. It would open doors she wouldn't be able to get close to on her own. She'd been willing to see Luke again, to put her pride on the line, to beg. But he was asking for much more than that.

"Is there any other way around this?" she asked hopefully.

"Not if you want that appointment."

"What all would this pretending entail?" she asked, still quite skeptical and not at all amused.

Was she seriously considering this craziness? Pretending to be engaged would require much more emotional work than she'd been willing to do when she first came in here. She actually hadn't even thought that Luke would require something in return, but he hadn't become a successful businessman by giving everything away.

Luke shrugged. "A few social-media posts, public appearances. You'd need to be here a few nights with me so everything seems authentic. Some PDA wouldn't hurt, either."

Public displays of affection? They wouldn't hurt? Kissing, touching, *pretending* would hurt. There was no way she could be in that type of situation and not recall everything she'd once dreamed of having with him and ultimately lost.

Damn it, he'd gotten shrewd since she'd left…

Okay, fine. She wanted this wedding. So she could play the game. She'd loved him once, so pretending to love him shouldn't be difficult. At least now, she knew how things would end. There wouldn't be naive stars in her eyes. She wouldn't lose her heart this time and she would stay in control. Besides, she'd be too busy planning the celebrity wedding of the year to get wrapped up with her ex, right?

"Fine." She moved closer to him and held out her hand. "It's a deal. And after the wedding, we're over. For good this time."

"Sounds good to me."

He took her hand and her heart began pounding. Her stomach knotted once again, and she knew in that instant that she was in trouble.

Playing her ex's pretend fiancée.

What the hell had she just gotten herself into?

Two

His brothers would no doubt give him hell over this, but the deal was done. Luke now had something he'd never wanted—a fiancée. Oh, when he and Cassandra had been together before, he'd bought the ring as a stepping stone, but he had never gotten up the courage to take that final step and actually propose. He just hadn't been sure, and then she'd left and he knew not asking her had been the right decision.

And now she was back and he was giving her everything she'd wanted before that he couldn't give. Well, pretending they had what she'd wanted. The entire situation was too ironic. Luke couldn't even wrap his mind around where the hell he'd come up with the idea, where the hell he'd lost control. Cassandra had swept in and presented her demands, and he'd been caught off guard so completely that he'd reacted without thinking.

Luke eased back in his leather desk chair and stared at the door that had slid closed after Cassandra's departure. She'd made one hell of an impact in such a short time, but Luke refused to admit he was anything but immune at this point. He'd been in love with her at one time, yes, but he hadn't been ready for a walk down the aisle. He still wasn't. She'd always wanted more than he could give.

Now, well… Who knew why he'd caved in to her demands. Or why he'd asked her to pretend to be his fiancée. True, he'd wanted the swarm of women to ease up ever since that damn article had been released. But, on the other hand, maybe he was trying to prove to himself that he had gotten over her, that she was nothing more than a memory from his past.

He sent Jake a text, asking him to find out where Cassandra was staying, how long she planned to be in town and everything else about her that he could find. Luke wanted to know all he could about his *fiancée*.

Within minutes, Luke's bodyguard informed him that she was staying just one floor below his bar, in the penthouse suite of The Beaumont. Fantastic. She was practically within touching distance. He sent a message to her room to be at The Cheshire tomorrow evening to play the role of his doting girlfriend.

And once everyone's initial shock wore off, they could discuss when and how to announce their...

Luke swallowed and pushed aside his frustrations.

Their engagement.

"Thank you so much for agreeing to meet with me."

Cassandra stepped inside Hannah Banks's lakeside three-story mansion and couldn't believe she was actually here. She'd listened to Hannah's music for years and the superstar was just as stunning in person as she was on television. Her smile seemed genuine and all the makeup and bling seemed to suit her over-the-top personality.

"Of course." Hannah closed the door and turned to face Cassandra and Luke. "I'm thrilled someone who knows Will is interested in taking part in our special day. I've been so swamped with work and with the new record, I haven't been able to zero in on anyone who really sees my vision. I know I want something quaint and quick, but I didn't think planning this would be so difficult."

There wasn't a doubt in Cassandra's mind that she would land this job. This would be her biggest undertaking, but the most rewarding and the most thrilling of her entire career.

"Sorry. I start chatting and can't stop. Come on out to the patio," Hannah stated as she started down a hallway leading to the back of the house. "I've got some drinks and Will is out there. I think he's on the phone, but he needs to finish up. I swear that man is always working."

"That's what we Sutherlands do," Luke chimed in. "I'm sure he'll be excited to take a break and discuss flowers and seating charts."

Cassandra smacked his abs as they walked through the home. "Hush. The groom should be part of the special day just as much as the bride."

"I agree." Hannah approached the patio doors and gestured for Cassandra and Luke to go first. "Looks like he's off the phone now."

Luke placed his hand on Cassandra's back and ushered her outside. Just that simple, dominating gesture had her shivering…and pulling away. She didn't want him to touch her. Not because she didn't enjoy it—she did, too much—but because she didn't want to get used to his strength or his affection. She didn't *want* to enjoy this.

True, they were going to pretend to be engaged, but they didn't have to start the show just yet. She wasn't sure what Luke was going to tell his brothers or his parents, but now wasn't the time to get in to that. First things first—land this dream job.

They hadn't exactly discussed when the faux engagement would begin, though he'd sent a message to her room that she should be at his bar tonight posing as his girlfriend.

Nothing like being summoned for affection. All of this was just as romantic and warm as the ending of their first go-round.

For now, though, she wasn't going to be overly doting on her ex. They would just have to speak in private later about the exact details of their in-public relationship.

"Will," Hannah said as she came around the furniture to stand beside her fiancé. "You know Cassandra."

Will's smile widened as he closed the gap between them and pulled her in for an embrace. She hadn't seen him in years, and he was still just as kind and handsome as she remembered. All of the Sutherland men were known for their Southern manners and sexy good looks, and a couple of the brothers had a reputation with the ladies, Gavin in particular. She wondered if he'd ever settled down or want some family life.

She'd wondered about all of them over the years and if the brothers had remained as close as they had been when she was around. Being an only child, Cassandra had always envied the bond these brothers shared. She'd been welcomed into the Sutherland fold just as if she'd always belonged there.

A twinge pinged at her heart and she had to ignore the yearning. This was not meant to be her family. That had been decided long ago and there was no turning back now.

"So great to see you again," Will said as he eased back. "You look great and you have a brand-new business. Sounds like life is treating you well."

Cassandra shifted her portfolio under her other arm and nodded as she stepped back. "I'm doing quite well. It seems so strange to be back in Beaumont Bay. It's grown even more since I left."

The shops, the bars, the homes—everything seemed to be on a bigger, grander scale than she remembered. Then again, the celebrities that had moved to this area had definitely made upgrades and they had certain expectations. Nashville was no longer the hottest spot or where the high-society folks went to play. There was no city that could compare to the nightlife and homes in Beaumont Bay around the lake and up into the hills.

"Please, sit." Hannah gestured to the large sectional. "Can I get you something to drink?"

"I'm fine, thank you."

Cassandra took a seat and the fact that Luke sat right next to her did nothing to help squash those growing nerves. They hadn't even gotten to the point of pretending to be a couple and he was already getting under her skin.

For now, she had a deal to seal and nothing else could bother her or get inside her head.

"I can't wait to see what you brought," Hannah said, beaming. "I have a few ideas of my own, but I haven't found anyone who shares the same vision."

"Well, I'm sure you will love what I've come up with and everything is negotiable. This is your wedding and I insist that all my clients be happy."

Cassandra placed the portfolio in her lap and flipped open the cover. She turned to show Will and Hannah, who were sitting across from her on another matching outdoor sofa. The glass table between them provided a perfect area to spread out the images and samples Cassandra had brought with her.

"The most important thing is for you both to enjoy your day and feel as if everything is flawless," Cassandra went on. "You should have no worries except how long you want to hold that kiss after you say 'I do.'"

Will laughed. "Oh, that will be all up to me."

Hannah elbowed him in the side and Cassandra saw how these two were made for each other. The way they looked into one another's eyes had her heart melting. She loved working with a couple in love, and sometimes, there were people that Cassandra could tell would actually make their marriage work. She could already see that Will and Hannah would definitely have their happily-ever-after.

"That is just about the only area I don't get involved in," Cassandra assured them. "I would like to start with the general overview. After doing some research, I understand the importance of privacy and I don't blame you one bit. I know Will values family, so I'm thinking something small, private yet stunning. I've drawn up two options for you to look at."

Cassandra slid easily into work mode. This was what she lived for, what kept her smiling and moving forward. Just because she'd lost the man she thought had been the love of her life didn't mean she'd stopped being a hopeless romantic. Seeing people found their soul mates, and knowing she had a part in making their dreams come true really was the best part of her life. She never felt like this was work; she was living out her own dream...even though she was going home alone at night after seeing happy couples getting started on their lives together.

As she flipped through the sample portfolio, Cassandra managed to push aside the fact that Luke was still sitting right next to her with his hip resting against hers.

Her emotions, their past, their current situation—none of those things mattered right now. All that mattered was wowing Hannah and Will with her ideas. Luke sat silently, but she knew he was listening and taking everything in.

She would have been fine had he not tagged along. She didn't trust him. She didn't want to spend more time with him than absolutely necessary. Considering this was his brother's wedding and the meeting had been set up through Luke, she supposed he deemed himself a vital part today.

"I'm amazed," Hannah finally said. She glanced to Will. "What do you think, babe? Which one of these sample ideas do you love?"

Will shook his head. "This is all pretty overwhelming."

Cassandra laughed. "It is at first, but we take everything one step at a time, and I won't pressure you or bombard you with questions or decision-making. This should be a fun process as we lead up to the big day. Even though we will be working at lightning speed, I will take the brunt of the stress. That's my job."

Hannah glanced back to the portfolio and flipped through again, pausing on the outdoor option with a sunset backdrop. Secretly, this was Cassandra's favorite, too, but she never offered her opinion unless asked.

"I've always dreamed of something outdoors," Hannah murmured. "The other designers I talked with urged me indoors in case of weather or for privacy, but I'd love to be out in the open."

Cassandra nodded. "We will take extra precautions with security, and as for the weather, we have beautiful tents that can be set up with chandeliers and draped in flowers so you won't even realize you're under a tent. But I always go in hopeful for a perfect outdoor wedding, so we won't think rain just yet."

Hannah smiled and tapped her polished red nail on the design. "This is what I want," she declared, looking back to Cassandra. "And I want you to be the one to make this happen."

A burst of elation and a swell of pride overcame her. Cassandra had believed she could get this wedding. That's why she'd dealt with the devil to get the meeting.

With a smile, Cassandra reached out her hand to Hannah. "I cannot wait to get started, and I promise you will be the happiest, most beautiful couple. This will be the wedding of the year."

Will sighed. "How hard is this going to hit my budget?"

Hannah elbowed him once again in his side. "*Our* budget, and I don't care. We're only getting married once."

He wrapped his arm around her shoulders and pulled her closer to his side. "You better only marry once. I'm it for you."

Luke got to his feet. "Okay, so if they're going to start this lovey-dovey stuff, I'm out of here."

Will glanced over to his brother. "Don't be jealous."

"Jealous?" Luke laughed. "I'm not jealous. Between you and Cash, something is in the water around here."

Cassandra had seen the news that their other brother, Cash, had gotten engaged during one of his concerts. The online photos she'd seen had been so damn romantic—the way he'd pulled his fiancée onto the stage and dropped the ring out of his guitar before proposing to a screaming crowd. Cassandra wouldn't be above asking to plan that epic wedding, too.

Will and Hannah stood, so Cassandra gathered her portfolio and also rose. She tucked it beneath her arm and glanced to Luke, whose eyes were locked onto hers.

"I'd say we're ready to go," she told him, then turned back to Will and Hannah. "I will be emailing you a detailed timeline. I don't want you all to be in the dark, even though some of the items are all on me. I would like to get together again in a couple days, or when it's good for you two, so we can get some of the larger things decided and pinned down since the wedding is in seven weeks."

Hannah nodded. "I'm free Wednesday morning, if that's okay? Do you want to meet here again?"

"Perfect." Cassandra pulled out her cell and made a note of the appointment. "I can't tell you how thrilling this is for me. I absolutely love your music."

Hannah beamed and smoothed her hair behind her ear. "That's so nice to hear. I'll be sure to get you some VIP tickets to my next concert. Where do you live?"

"I live in Kentucky, actually."

"Oh, well, I'll be doing a couple of shows there. We'll work something out."

Cassandra couldn't believe how perfect this day had gone. Hannah Banks was just as sweet in private as she'd seemed in public. This wedding would be such a fun and a rewarding event to work on. And hopefully Cassandra would be so busy with this project, she wouldn't have too much time to devote to her "fiancé."

Once they were back in Luke's truck, he pulled out of Hannah's drive. Cassandra smoothed her hair over one shoulder and adjusted her sunglasses against the bright sky.

"You're really good at your job," he said.

Cassandra glanced over to Luke, who was keeping his eyes on the road. "You sound surprised."

"Not surprised at all, actually," he admitted. "I knew you'd be amazing at this. I've just never seen you in your element before."

A little taken aback by his admission, Cassandra smiled. "Well, thanks. I love my job and I always think that if you're doing what you love, then it never feels like work."

"I agree. Owning bars was always my goal. I love the atmosphere, the people… Well, I did love the people until I was bombarded with women ready for me to make them Mrs. Sutherland."

A burst of jealousy surged through her, but that was ridiculous. She had no claim to Luke and it wasn't like the man hadn't dated over the years. Maybe he'd even had a serious relationship. None of that was her business or concern, which was why she shouldn't be thinking of it.

When Luke pulled in front of The Beaumont, where she had rented the penthouse for the next few months, he killed the engine and stepped out. Before she could get her own door, Luke had opened it and reached his hand inside.

Cassandra shifted her gaze to his and found that intense stare looking back at her. She slid her hand into his and there was no ignoring the familiar jolt that had always aroused her. Apparently, now was no different than eight years ago.

When she stepped out of the truck, he didn't move back, and instead he caged her against the opening and smiled.

"What are you doing?" she murmured as their bodies pressed together. Instant bursts of arousal coursed through her and she cursed herself for allowing herself to feel such worthless emotions.

"Practicing."

And that was all the warning she got before his mouth descended onto hers.

Three

What the hell was he doing?

Well, he knew what he was doing. He was finally kissing Cassandra after an entire day of fantasizing about it. But what was he thinking? There were no cameras around, no one to care that he was kissing his ex.

No, this kiss was purely selfish and completely wrong...and also so damn perfect. He was supposed to be proving the point that he was over her and had absolutely no interest. Yet here he was, wondering what else remained the same...because his reaction to kissing sure as hell had.

Cassandra sighed into him, her body practically

melting against his. Luke shored up every ounce of resolve not to touch her anywhere else. Gripping her waist would be so easy, but he'd already lost his mind and kissed her.

She pressed a hand to his chest and leaned away. "Luke."

Muttering a curse beneath his breath, he took a step back and kept his eyes locked on her. She blinked up at him and licked her lips, clearly waiting for an explanation.

"I figured we should get the first kiss out of the way," he explained.

"We've shared thousands of kisses."

As if he needed the reminder. Luke was well aware of his experience with Cassandra and that's why he couldn't stop himself. Okay, so, fine. They'd kissed and he'd liked it. But now it was out of his system…right? He could ignore his sexual desires.

Luke berated himself. He was a damn fool for coming up with this plan—for kissing her, and for asking her to pretend to be his fiancée—but now he was in it. At least his wild idea would calm the masses after that article.

"I didn't want our first kiss in eight years to be in front of people," he told her. "Just in case things were awkward."

Cassandra laughed. "Awkward? Luke, every bit of this is awkward, but I want this wedding and now that I have it, I'll hold up my end of the deal. But no more kissing when we don't have to. No touching, no nothing."

Oh, but he wanted to…and he likely would ask her again when they were alone because she'd melted against him and clearly craved that physical connection, just as he did.

Did she expect him to deny them both when it was clear she enjoyed it just as much? Had she not melted against him and returned that kiss with just as much desire and passion as he was feeling?

"What time do you want me at The Cheshire tonight?" she asked.

Considering her penthouse was just below his rooftop bar, he fully planned on picking her up and taking her with him.

"I'll get you at seven and we'll have dinner before we head to the bar."

"Dinner?" she asked, quirking an eyebrow.

Luke couldn't help but smile. "All part of the ruse, Cass."

Her lids lowered a fraction and he realized he'd used her nickname. It suited the girl he used to know, but *Cassandra* definitely fit the woman he'd seen working her wedding magic earlier today. There was a new side to her now—an intriguing side that he had to ignore. Just because they had a past and now a faux relationship didn't mean he needed to dig deeper into her life and find out all that had happened since she'd left.

Once he'd picked up the pieces of his heart and concentrated on what he could actually control, Luke had found he was a happy man. He didn't need love, or whatever that emotion was people claimed to feel. He didn't need marriage. This chapter of his life right now was the happiest he'd ever been, so there was absolutely no need to look elsewhere to fill voids that weren't there. He'd filled all of those voids with a hefty bank account and loyal friends.

"Fine," she conceded. "I'll be ready at seven."

Luke stepped out of the way and let her pass. He watched as she went through the glass doors into the hotel and felt a little twinge of pain when she didn't look back. It was quite the parallel to when she'd left years ago and hadn't even given him a second glance.

A few hours without being around Cassandra had helped Luke get his head on straight before seeing her again tonight. There was no room in his life for him to get caught up in her again.

When she'd left town eight years ago, he hadn't been quite ready to propose. He'd had too much tied up in all of his start-up businesses. And then when she'd left, Luke figured he was better off without her. He'd been such a fool, but not anymore.

That was all in the past, and he'd certainly learned from his mistakes. He'd never let anyone get that close to him again and he'd managed to build the life and career he'd dreamed of for so long. He couldn't be totally upset about how things had turned out.

Obviously, he and Cassandra weren't meant to be and that had just taken some time to sink in.

Luke pulled in a breath and stepped off the elevator at the penthouse level. There was only one door, but Luke knew the chime sounded inside her room because the private elevator indicated when there was a guest. Just as he started to knock, the door flung open and Luke nearly gasped, but managed to suppress his reaction…barely.

She stood before him in hip-hugging black leather pants, a pair of black heels and a dark red halter with a very low scoop neck that left nothing to the imagination and showed off all of that mocha skin he craved to touch.

Gone was the professional woman from earlier who'd been wearing a sundress and classy sandals with minimal makeup. Now, those red lips and dark eyes tempted him in a whole new way. He wanted to lean in and see how much he could mess that up, but he remained still.

What the hell game was she playing?

She was still smiling that almost innocent smile and she had that perkiness about her that just drew

people in. Cassandra was like a magnetic force…
and he refused to be drawn in.

"This outfit will certainly get attention."

Cassandra held out her arms and did a slow
spin. "That was the whole idea, right?" she asked
as she came back around. "You wanted people to
notice you're taken."

Yeah, he did, but at what expense? Because he
still needed to be able to work and to function.
With this damn outfit, he'd be lucky if he could
string two coherent sentences together.

From the smirk on her face, she knew exactly
the effect she had on him and she was loving every
minute of it. She was a vixen. That's exactly what
Cassandra Taylor was, and he had nobody to blame
but himself. Maybe he should have just stuck with
the women bombarding him for dates and marriage. At least he could control that situation, even
if he'd found it annoying and overwhelming.

"Let's head on up," he told her as he stepped
aside so she could come out into the hallway. "I've
had the chef prepare our dinner and it's ready in
the private back VIP room."

"Don't you have customers there?" she asked.

"Only a few and that's the point." He punched
the elevator button and waited. "We want to be
seen, but not seeming to be throwing it in their
faces. It will look even more authentic if people
think we're to trying to keep this quiet."

They stepped onto the elevator. Luke was glad they were only going up one floor because he was too tempted to push the stop button and practice those kisses again. There was no way in hell she was immune to this sexual tension. It was as if she'd chose this outfit and that sultry lipstick to torment him even further.

"A secret fake engagement," she murmured. "Sounds like a lot of work."

"That's the price you agreed to pay," he reminded her.

Though at this point, he felt like he was paying a greater price.

Luke had to shift his focus to something else. Maybe to the fact that he'd let her go once and she blamed him for their breakup. If he kept telling himself that this was the same woman who'd broken him so many years ago, that should be more than enough to make him see that he'd been lucky to have her step away from his life. He'd refused to beg back then and he wouldn't be doing any begging now, no matter how much he'd enjoyed that damn kiss.

As they stepped into the rooftop bar, Cassandra glanced around. He let her walk on ahead, as she clearly wanted to see the space. She'd only been here once before, when she'd first come by his office to ask her favor. Luke waited as she walked through and glanced around at the high-top tables for mingling, the low leather sofas for cozying, the stage where there were nightly performances, and the long bar that was home to the best bartender in all of Tennessee.

Luke was proud of everything he'd accomplished. True, he'd lost Cassandra in the process, but that was all in the past and she'd made that choice clear. This bar, and his others, were his present and future. His workers were like family and he had his brothers. With Will and Cash's fiancées, he was gaining two new sisters. His life was full.

So why did he still feel a hole that he couldn't quite explain?

A few customers were hanging out at the hightop tables, where there were no seats. He found that some people wanted to stand and some preferred more intimacy, which was why he'd installed the outdoor sofas and the small tables with club chairs. His goal from day one had been to create an atmosphere where everyone could feel comfortable and offer his customers a place to come and enjoy the amazing music he prided himself on offering.

In a few hours, especially once the band showed up, this rooftop would be flooded with patrons. The food and drinks would be passed around and that's when Luke truly loved his job—he loved getting to know the people of the town and the surrounding areas.

"This is really amazing," Cassandra said as she came back to him. "I'd seen pictures online, but was too focused yesterday to pay too much attention. Everything is truly stunning, from the atmosphere to the views."

The views were indeed breathtaking and one of the main reasons he'd chosen to open a rooftop bar. Seeing the city lights of Beaumont Bay and the homes in the distance that surrounded the lake, nestled between mountain peaks like a big city, was definitely unique. This area was undeniably the place to be, and over the past few years, the Bay had really blown up with the arrival of real-estate moguls, high-rollers, artists and country-music transplants, who all wanted even better nightlife and larger homes than they had in Nashville.

"Are you ready for dinner?" he asked.

Cassandra nodded and crossed back to him. With his hand on the small of her back, Luke led her to the private VIP area that was in the back behind one-way-mirrored walls. They slid open and shut as soon as they were inside.

"Swanky like your office with all these hidden walls," she murmured. "Maybe I should've dressed up a little more."

His hand slid around to the dip in her waist as he eased her against his side and leaned down to whisper in her ear.

"This is more than sexy enough."

Her body shivered beneath his touch and that's precisely the reaction he wanted her to have. He wanted her to remember all the amazing times they'd had together, both in public and in private.

While he'd moved on successfully and happily, maybe there was a thread of payback in this plan that he hadn't realized until now. He didn't want to be an ass, but there was nothing wrong with showing her exactly what she'd missed out on by leaving.

Luke didn't give her time to reply as he ushered her over to the corner booth where he'd had their meal set up. Luke hoped her tastes hadn't changed too much over the years because he'd gone with her favorites from the main restaurant downstairs.

Once Cassandra was seated, Luke slid in beside her and purposely eased his thigh right alongside hers. She wasn't immune to him, like she wanted to be. She wouldn't have melted against him with that kiss if she had been. Besides, it was just a simple touch, right?

"You're practically on my lap," she muttered as she glanced between them and then up to his face.

Luke smiled. "I feel like you're not taking your role as doting fiancée seriously."

"I feel like you're purposely being difficult."

He shrugged. "Too late to back out. We had an agreement."

Her eyes narrowed and Luke ignored her anger. There was a fine line between anger and arousal, and right now, he was on one side and she was on the other. He knew just where to touch her, just what to say, to pull her over to his side...or, at the very least, to meet him in the middle.

Yet here he was, trying to play all noble, as if he didn't want to strip her down and see if they were just as good together as they'd been before. There wasn't a doubt in Luke's mind that they would be just as hot, if not hotter.

Damn, he could use a physical release, but he wasn't going to go that far...not with Cassandra. He wasn't a masochist. He wouldn't be hurt by her again. And despite how they'd ended, he still respected women and would never be such a jerk.

Cassandra turned her focus back to the table. "So what are we having? I'm starving."

That was one thing he remembered. She'd always had a hearty appetite, and he had really loved that about her. She wasn't one to shy away from what she wanted, or worry about carbs and all that. Cassandra had so much confidence, she had such a love for life... He'd naively thought they could have some grand dynasty with his businesses.

Looking back, maybe he had been selfish, maybe he hadn't seen how important her own goals had been because he'd been so busy with his own. He hadn't thought she would just up and leave him, though. That harsh action on her part had proven they weren't meant to be together. If they were, she would have stayed, or they would have found a way back to each other…and not in some warped fake manner.

"I had them prepare bacon-wrapped sliders, some crab cakes and there is some grilled asparagus."

She started removing the domed lids and she literally moaned right there. Moaned. As if he needed another reaction from her to turn him on.

"Eat as much as you want. I had a late lunch and I'm fine with beer."

She reached for a slider and set it on her plate. "What beers do you have on tap? Local ones, I presume."

"I try to support local as much as possible, but I also keep up with the demand of more well-known brands, too. There is a demographic that doesn't like the IPA or craft beers and prefers the more traditional."

"Give me your favorite local draft," she told him with a smile.

Luke jerked slightly. "I didn't think you liked beer."

Cassandra shrugged and her smile widened. "There's quite a bit you don't know about me now. I'm not the same girl I used to be."

Clearly, she wasn't. With that revelation, a

part of him wanted to uncover all the ways she'd changed. First off, she drank beer, which was surprising. She'd never liked any type of alcohol before, always saying it tasted bitter.

"Do you prefer a fruity beer or something stout?" he asked.

"Surprise me," she countered with that saucy, flirty grin.

Now that was the old Cassandra he knew. She used to love surprises and he had always enjoyed giving them. Spontaneity had been one of the main components of their relationship. They'd been happy once. Hell, he'd been happy up until the moment she'd left. He hadn't seen that coming and the bitterness had consumed him for much too long after she'd gone.

Now she was back and he hadn't even realized he wanted the chance to prove he was over her, but he was getting the opportunity. He'd prove that he'd been just fine without her, and would continue to be fine without her. And if he got a sliver of payback at the same time, then so be it.

Luke glanced to his VIP-room bartender and that's all it took for Miles to come over and promptly take their orders. After deciding on a couple of flights for Cassandra to try, Luke ordered his favorite pilsner.

Just as the drinks arrived, Cassandra let out a gasp and grabbed her cell. Luke glanced over to see her fingers flying over the screen, and she kept muttering.

Intrigued, Luke curled his hands around his chilled stein and watched her. She continued to talk to herself, something about catering and seating charts.

After several minutes, she slid her phone back into her purse and turned toward him.

"So, tell me what we have here," she said as she gestured toward the flights.

Luke laughed. "What was all that about?"

"What?"

"The phone, the self-chatter. Do you do that often?"

"Oh, um, yes." She shrugged and turned back to survey the flights. She chose the palest first. "When I think of something for work, I need to get it into my notes or I'll completely forget it. There's too much swirling around in my mind for me to possibly remember everything I have going on."

"And something inspired you from being here and ordering beer?" he asked.

Cassandra threw him a glance. "I get inspiration from everywhere."

Interesting. He wanted to dig deeper into that mind of hers. He wanted to know what made her think of his brother's wedding while they were on a pretend date. Did she ever insert elements into others' weddings that she wanted in her own? Did she even want to get married anymore?

Why was his mind even wandering to those questions? He didn't care about her personal life. The only reason he'd come up with this fake engagement was to get some relief from the women bombarding him since he'd been named the most eligible bachelor in the area. Working had become difficult when all he'd been able to do was pose for selfies, have phone numbers slipped into his pockets, and get propositioned. While that was all great as an ego boost, he really did need to focus on work, and he sure as hell wasn't looking to add a Mrs. to his Mr.

A flash of red hair and a tight dress caught the corner of his eye and Luke glanced around for a split second before dread settled in his gut. Quickly, he slid his arm along the back of the booth behind Cassandra. She turned to him, her eyes darting to his mouth as he leaned in closer.

"What—?"

His lips covered hers, and once again, she seemed to fall right in tune with him as she met his kiss with a demand of her own. The passion was instant and strong, which was why he knew if they attempted a temporary fling, it might be dangerous, but they would both thoroughly enjoy themselves.

Cassandra's hand slid along his thigh as she eased closer and opened her lips for him. She might tell him that she'd changed over the years, but this was still the same passionate woman he'd enjoyed years ago.

Luke tipped his head and reached up, cupping her jaw and seeking more. Damn, the woman could kiss, and there wasn't a thing in this world that could make him stop...

"She's gone, sir."

Except the sound of his bodyguard.

Luke broke the kiss and turned his focus to Jake, who merely nodded and then slipped away.

"What—what was that?" Cassandra panted.

"A woman was walking this way with her eyes on me," Luke murmured, still trying to catch his own breath.

Cassandra smoothed her hair away from her face. "Oh, right. Our *relationship*."

Yeah, exactly. She'd forgotten about the ruse and for a brief moment, so had he. Those kisses, all two that they'd shared so far, were already getting to him...

How in the hell was he supposed to keep pretending? Every single part of him wanted her, wanted more than this farce. True, he'd set the terms, but he needed a redo and he needed to add in a hell of a lot more than kisses here and there.

"I'm going to need a heads-up before you come in for the attack next time," she murmured.

With his arm still behind her back, Luke shifted his body to angle more toward her.

"Attack?" he whispered. "You were more than a willing participant, in both instances."

Cassandra pursed her lips. "So what? You're a good kisser. That doesn't mean I don't need a second to process before it happens."

"Fine," he conceded. "What word do you want me to say before I kiss you?"

She seemed to think for a half second before a grin spread across her face. That grin should've scared the hell out of him because the woman looked like she was about to make him regret that question.

"Sorry."

Luke blinked. "Excuse me."

"I'd like you to say 'sorry' before you kiss me next time."

Of all the things he thought she'd say, "sorry" certainly wasn't one of them.

"Why would I do that?" he asked.

"Because you asked what I wanted and that's it." She scooted away just a fraction and took a drink of the next beer in her sample lineup. "This is delicious. I definitely love this one the best so far. It's smooth, but still full of flavor."

As he sat and listened to her discuss her beer, he realized that he'd lost control here—she'd just successfully laid down another rule. Damn it. He really wasn't sure he was going to come out the other side of this unscathed.

Unless he set a few rules of his own.

Four

Cassandra maneuvered through her computer-generated layout, still not happy with the arrangement of the decor. Even though this was Plan B, in case of inclement weather, it had to be just as perfect as the main plan.

She stood up from the desk in her penthouse and stretched her arms over her head. She'd gotten in late last night after spending several hours at The Cheshire with Luke. She couldn't deny that she'd had a great time and had seen him in his element. People loved him, especially the ladies.

Cassandra also couldn't deny the surge of jealousy that had stayed with her all night. Too many women had tried to slip Luke their numbers or get their picture with the Most Eligible Bachelor. No way did Cassandra dare walk away from him, or she'd never hear the end of how she hadn't kept up her side of the bargain. She'd stuck by his side all night, just like any devoted fiancée would have.

Luke had kept his arm around her waist most of the night and one time even slid his hand into hers, but there had been no more kisses. Maybe because he didn't want to use the code word, but she smiled every time she thought about him having to apologize before kissing her next time.

Cassandra went to the minibar and poured a glass of pinot, then turned back to the balcony doors and stared out at the sunset. This was such a gorgeous view and she felt comfortable here, even though this was all temporary. For the next few months, this was going to be her home.

She wasn't sure if she'd settled in so easily because she'd grown up in Beaumont Bay, or if seeing Luke and Will had pulled her back to the good times in her past. She wasn't sure what would happen once she saw the entire Sutherland crew. They'd been like family to her, but she had to expect the flood of memories—she just hoped she didn't get too swept up in the ambiance of the wedding and the tight bond of the brothers and their parents.

Travis and Dana Sutherland were the quintessential couple who worked hard to show their children how to make their way through life. Travis was the most popular real-estate mogul in Beaumont Bay and the surrounding area. He'd hoped one of his sons would take him up on the idea of joining the family business, but all four boys had loved music in one way or another. Cassandra knew they each had gone in that direction in their own way.

Cassandra took a sip of her wine and reminded herself once again that she was only back here on business…and those kisses were just business, too. All part of the temporary arrangement to get the boost she needed as she set off on her own in a high-profile industry.

This would all work out and the sacrifice to her sanity would be worth it. Besides, it wasn't like she didn't enjoy kissing Luke. The man was impossible to ignore and she couldn't deny her attraction to him. But attraction didn't mean she had to take action. She could kiss him, hold hands, even snuggle a little, and still remain emotionally detached.

Right? She just couldn't get too wrapped up in the Sutherland family because they had been so damn difficult to leave the first time. She'd missed them so much and had felt like she'd broken many relationships, not just the one with Luke.

With another sip of wine, Cassandra turned to the piano next to the wall of windows overlooking the city. She couldn't believe it when she'd come into the penthouse and spotted this beauty. About seven years ago she'd taken up the hobby of playing, needing something to occupy her time when she wasn't working. Coming home to an empty space after being in a relationship for so long had been way too quiet, way too lonely. It had started taking a mental toll on her, so she'd taken up the piano and fallen in love.

It had taken her a long time to get over the heartache of Luke Sutherland. Learning the piano had been so relaxing, giving her a creative outlet that only she knew about. That way there was no criticism, no right or wrong way. She just enjoyed herself, and over the years she'd actually gotten pretty good.

Cassandra set her glass of wine on the top of the piano and took a seat at the white bench. She lifted the piano lid and stared down at the ebony and ivory keys before delicately placing her fingertips over them. Instantly, she closed her eyes as her hands traveled, a familiar tune filling the open space, immediately soothing her soul.

When she finished with one song, she eased right into another, humming along as she allowed the music to whisk her away. Cassandra didn't know how long she played—all she knew was she needed the mental break and nothing relaxed her like the piano.

She played the final note of the song, then pulled in a deep breath and opened her eyes. Movement from her peripheral vision had her jerking around on the bench.

"Sorry, just me."

Cassandra came to her feet, her heart beating fast. "What the hell are you doing in here? How did you get in?"

"I buzzed for you to let me in," Luke explained. "I heard the piano, so I guess you didn't hear me. When did you learn to play? That was amazing."

Crossing her arms over her chest, Cassandra narrowed her eyes. "Answer my question first. How did you get in here?"

He just stared at her like she was silly for asking. He might be powerful and own the bar space and be chummy with the owners and managers of The Beaumont, but that didn't mean he could do whatever he wanted.

This nonchalant manner of his had to go...and so did his line of thinking.

"You can't just let yourself in," she scolded. "What if I'd just gotten out of the shower?"

His eyes traveled over her body and she realized she'd said the exact wrong thing. No doubt that would have made him even more excited.

"I've seen all you have," he reminded her. "And I didn't mean to creep you out by letting myself in. I just assumed you couldn't hear me."

"Well, I still deserve respect and privacy," she retorted. "We're just pretending, remember? I need my own space, Luke. What are you doing here, anyway?"

He shook his head. "I answered your question, now answer mine. When did you learn to play like that?"

"When you crushed my heart and I moved away. I needed something to occupy my time so I picked up a hobby."

Luke's lips thinned as the muscles in his jaw ticked. He took a step toward her, and then another, until all that was between them was the piano bench.

Cassandra held her ground and never looked away from that expressive stare that had her pinned and mesmerized. She'd always loved his dark eyes, which were framed by even darker lashes. Now he also had a close-cropped beard that only added to his sexy, rugged allure. He looked nothing like the billionaire he'd come to be and maybe that's why she was having such a difficult time focusing. She kept seeing the young man he used to be, but she was also fascinated by the man he'd become.

"Crushed your heart?" he repeated. "Maybe you don't remember exactly how things went down."

Seriously? Was he honestly trying to play the victim here?

Cassandra reached for her glass of wine and

took a sip, realizing it had gotten warm. She was definitely going to need to refresh her glass.

"I'm not rehashing the past." She turned and headed toward the bar in the corner, putting some much-needed distance between them. "That's not why I came back to town and what's done is done."

She refilled her glass and turned back to face him. Thankfully, the bar top now separated them. "Now, what are you doing here?" she asked again.

"I wanted to know if you would like to come up tonight," he told her. "I have a new band that sounds amazing and I think they're really going to hit it big. They have some interest from Nashville and I invited Will tonight to listen to them and hopefully offer them a deal."

Luke seemed pretty excited about this group, which made her smile. Despite how they'd parted years ago, and their current turmoil, Luke had really grown something remarkable with his businesses. She had to admit a sliver of her was jealous, but that was ridiculous. How could she be jealous of a thing? Of course, he was proud of all he'd accomplished, and he should be. Being jealous at this stage in the game was both childish and unreasonable.

Besides, she'd moved on, as well, so anything she felt now was just residual and had no place in the present.

"That sounds like fun, but I really need to work

so I can be prepared when I meet with Hannah again."

Luke leaned against the glossy bar top, flattening his palms on the marble. "You were so damn prepared when we were there last, you were all but ordained to do the ceremony yourself."

Cassandra pursed her lips and thought. "You know, that's not a bad idea."

"I'm being serious. You can come up for a bit to make an appearance. It's important."

Cassandra sighed. "And your work is more important than mine?"

Maybe nothing had changed after all. Still battling over careers and emotions, just like old times. At least now she knew the outcome and wouldn't be blindsided.

Luke growled and eased around the bar to stand right next to her. She shifted her body so she could gaze up into those captivating eyes. He'd always been able to persuade her with just a look, but she was in charge now and no sexy glance or cute words or even toe-curling kisses could get her to give in. This wedding was too important to her and would most certainly be career-changing, which was precisely what she needed for her brand-new company.

"Just for an hour," he commanded. "You can stay for an hour."

Cassandra wanted to give in. She wanted to

go hang out and have a drink and listen to music and unwind, but that wouldn't help her try to figure out the details for Hannah and Will's big day. They'd entrusted her to make this the best day of their lives and not even Cassandra's attraction to Luke Sutherland would make her lose sight of that responsibility.

"As much as it sounds like fun, I can't."

Luke continued to stare until she realized he was leaning in closer...and closer still.

"Wh-what are you doing?" she murmured.

His hand slid along her jawline and Cassandra couldn't help herself as she leaned into his touch. Then when his thumb raked over her bottom lip, she closed her eyes and instinctively touched the tip of her tongue to his skin.

"I'm just getting to know you again," he answered, his voice husky from arousal.

More like trying to seduce her again...and, damn it, it was working.

"There's no need for that." She pulled in a shaky breath and willed herself not to lean in and kiss him. "You know me well enough to pull off this fake engagement."

The back of his fingertips feathered over her jawline, along the column of her neck and down to the V of her shirt before he pulled away slowly, methodically.

"Maybe I still find you attractive," he countered. "Maybe I'm done denying my wants…and your wants."

She stared up into his eyes. "You have to deny everything. What we're doing is nothing more than a temporary sham."

"Perhaps," he agreed, then leaned in closer until his mouth was a breath from hers. "Or maybe while we're together, we should explore this."

"This?"

His warm breath tickled her face and she wished he'd just close that distance and put her out of her misery. She could finish this and take what she wanted, but considering she was telling him this wasn't a great idea, she'd just be contradicting herself.

"We're adults, Cass. We're still drawn to each other. There's nothing wrong with acting on that and realizing exactly what this is…and what it isn't."

She blinked up at him and forced herself to take a step back before she lost her mind and gave in to everything he was offering—gave in to everything her body so desired.

"There's everything wrong with it," she countered. "I can't get wrapped up in you any more than I already have."

His eyes held hers for a second before he nodded. "Then I'll let you get back to work."

Without another word, he turned and let himself

out. Cassandra stared at the door long after he was gone, wondering how the hell he'd been inside her penthouse for so short a time, yet had made such a sizable impact on her every thought.

She also wondered what had made him leave and finally accept her rejection. Had she wounded his pride? Did he finally see that pushing forward on some temporary fling was a terrible idea?

One thing was certain—Cassandra knew Luke well enough to know that once he set his mind to something, he wasn't about to give up...and that meant he would be back. He would try to convince her they could still be good together.

She had to be ready to resist.

Five

She was a damn fool. When she should have been in her penthouse working on the wedding, Cassandra found herself hanging out in the back of the crowd, listening to the new band Luke had introduced thirty minutes ago.

He'd been right. The band was amazing and no doubt they'd be a hit one day soon.

Luke had also been right that she should be here. Enjoying music at his bar was better than worrying and second-guessing herself with her work.

Maybe it was the almost kiss. Maybe it was the way he'd stroked her jawline. Or perhaps the way he'd looked at her, as if he actually needed her in the most primal way.

No matter what had gotten her up to the rooftop, she couldn't deny that memories were intertwining with present emotions and she had no idea how she was going to handle all of it.

After he'd left, she'd taken a few minutes to battle with herself over what to do, but she couldn't stay in that penthouse with her thoughts and her sexual frustrations.

Cassandra had changed clothes, thrown her hair into a messy bun, added some mascara and gloss, and found herself up at The Cheshire.

As she glanced around the crowd, she noted many people smiling, drinking, nodding their heads to the catchy beat of the music. She saw Will back in the corner with Hannah tucked in at his side.

Cassandra made her way over and realized Cash and Gavin were seated on the couch across from Will and Hannah. Well, the entire Sutherland clan was here, and she assumed the lady between Gavin and Cash was Cash's fiancée, Presley.

Maybe she shouldn't have started walking that way, but it was too late to turn around because Will caught her eye and immediately waved her over. That motion caught the attention of everyone else and they all turned to see who was coming.

With a smile in place, Cassandra maneuvered

through the crowd. Will came to his feet when she got to the sofa.

"Luke didn't tell us you'd be here." He greeted her with a hug. "Have a seat."

"I told him I was working, but I wanted to take a break." Cassandra eased down onto the couch where Will had vacated his seat. He went to sit on the other side of Hannah.

"So, how is everything coming along?" Hannah asked with a gleam in her eye. "You don't know how excited I am."

Not nearly as excited as Cassandra was as she worked on this once-in-a-lifetime dream wedding.

"It's all she's talked about," Will stated. "You've created a bridezilla."

Hannah laughed as she slapped his chest before turning her attention back to Cassandra. "I'm not a bridezilla. I'm just so thrilled that someone knew my vision better than I could ever explain."

Cassandra smiled and then turned her attention to the other sofa, where Cash was staring at her.

"Hey, Cash," she greeted. "It's been a long time."

"It has, and apparently things have picked right back up where you all left off." He continued to stare at her with an unsettling gaze. "Rumor is you and Luke are engaged."

"What?"

"You are?"

Will and Hannah had spoken up at the same time. Cassandra's breath caught in her throat and she wished like hell Luke would've given her a heads-up as to what he'd told—or not told—his brothers. Then again, he'd been busy sneaking into her penthouse and trying to seduce her.

"That's what I saw online," Cash laughed. "So who knows."

Why hadn't she and Luke discussed what they'd tell his brothers? Or why hadn't he addressed this with them to begin with? Now she was stuck in an awkward spot. Did she go along with this or deny it?

But their whole plan had been to pretend to be engaged, right? So she went with it.

"Actually, we are," Cassandra announced. "It's new—you can ask Luke about all the details, but we didn't say anything because we really didn't want to take away from Hannah and Will, or Cash and Presley."

"Nothing would take away from any of that," Hannah exclaimed. "I can't believe you guys didn't say anything when you were at the house. This is so exciting."

Well, Cassandra wouldn't quite put that bold label on the moment, but she was on shaky ground here and really wished they could talk about something else.

"Where's your ring?" Will asked, his eyes darting to her left hand. "Don't let Luke skimp on that. He's frugal, but come on."

"That last one he picked out wasn't as big as what he could afford now," Cash joked.

"The last one?" Cassandra asked. If she thought her nerves were shot before, that was nothing compared to the effect of this bombshell.

Cash nodded. "When you two were together before. He'd asked Mom to help him look for one in his price range. He ended up with a pearl with diamonds or something like that. Do you remember, Will? It wasn't traditional."

Cassandra's heart pounded. Luke had gotten her a ring before? Why had he never said anything? He knew she wanted to marry him, that she'd left because he wouldn't do just that. How could he let her walk away without a word? What the hell? He couldn't have come to her and told her what he'd planned—that he had a *ring*?

She had so many questions, but asking them would only result in thrusting her back into the past and nothing good would come from that.

Besides, the more she tossed this new fact around in her head, the angrier she became…which wasn't good for either of them. She wasn't in town to analyze everything that had gone wrong in the past. Too many years had passed, and quite honestly, she wasn't the same woman anymore, and it was obvious Luke wasn't the same guy. The man she'd fallen in love with would never play games. He would have been totally transparent and open. So what had happened?

"Oh, yeah. He'd put all his money into starting the bars," Will replied, pulling her from her thoughts. "We gave him hell over such a small ring, but he refused to take money from anyone."

As the brothers went back and forth about the ring and what ancestor the piece belonged to, Cassandra scanned the rooftop area as her mind raced. Through the variety of people mingling, drinking and dancing to the music, she finally spotted her faux fiancé.

Luke smiled and nodded as two twentysomething ladies were talking to him. One of the women placed her hand on his arm and threw her head back in a dramatic, nearly pathetic laugh for attention. Jealousy hit Cassandra hard, so she excused herself from the group and made her way through the crowd.

She had no idea why this whole scene pissed her off, but if they were going to fake a relationship, then that's what they needed to do. Aside from the women hanging on him—oh, and now trying to get a selfie with him—Cassandra was still reeling from the revelation that Luke had gotten a ring for her when they'd been together.

Without even an "excuse me," Cassandra slid between the women and her "fiancé." With her arm around his waist, she glanced up at him, loving that surprised look on his face.

"Hey, babe," she greeted. "Sorry I kept you waiting."

"I thought you had to work," he stated, clearly shocked she was here.

She smiled, though she gritted her teeth to keep from lashing out…which was ridiculous. She had no reason to be jealous. None. Luke was a sexy, successful man and Cassandra knew full well he'd been with women since they'd ended things. But having the fact shoved in her face didn't sit so well with her.

"Nothing is more important than spending time with my fiancé," she declared, purposely pouring on the fake affection.

"Wait," one of the ladies said. "You're engaged?"

Cassandra glanced to them, pretending she'd just realized they were so close. She really should earn an award for her acting skills.

"Oh, how rude of me." She extended her hand. "I'm Cassandra Taylor, Luke's fiancée. And you two are friends of Lukie's?"

Lukie?

She hadn't meant to sound that fake, but she also knew that nickname would tick off Luke, so she couldn't help but be a little giddy. Okay, fine. She was petty. This whole situation had obviously caused her to override her common sense, but she couldn't rein it back in at this point.

"We actually just met," one of the women said. "We didn't know he was engaged."

"It's still fairly new," Cassandra explained. "We dated years ago and I just got back into town and we realized we couldn't live without each other."

Luke's arm slid around her and his hand came to rest on the curve of her hip.

"So, you see, ladies, that's why I couldn't do the selfie," he told them. "I have nothing but respect for my girl here."

His girl. At one time she'd loved when he called her that. And there was still a sliver of excitement and a little arousal that slid through her at the declaration.

She really should have just stayed in her penthouse. Then she wouldn't have been in the company of the Sutherland brothers' crew, learned about the ring, or gotten jealous over two very young women talking to Luke.

This was what he did, though. He mingled, chatted with the customers, flirted. He was just being typical charming Luke. How could she fault him for being in his natural state?

"If you'll excuse us, ladies. Please, continue to enjoy the show and the drinks."

Luke smiled to the duo and eased Cassandra away. She kept her arm around him as he guided her toward the back hallway behind the bar. He tapped in the code and the wall door slid open to reveal his hidden office.

She had too many questions, not to mention the unwanted possessiveness she'd felt when she obviously had no real claim on Luke. There was nothing other than a superficial business deal going on between them and she would do well to remember that from here on out.

The wall slid closed after they stepped inside and Luke came to stand in front of her. He shoved his hands in the pockets of his jeans and stared down at her as if waiting on some explanation.

The silence curled around them, the force of it almost magnetic as she found herself taking a step toward him. She really didn't know where to start, but he finally broke the tension and saved her from opening up.

"What happened to work?" he asked.

"I needed a break."

"I heard you say that before, but what's the real reason?"

She had needed a break. She also wanted to see the bar and enjoy the atmosphere and the band, and maybe she wanted to see Luke again in his element. She couldn't just turn off her attraction, nor could she turn off her curiosity.

Cassandra pulled in a shaky breath and stepped

back, away from those intense eyes and that powerful stare.

"We need to get our story straight because your brother just asked about our engagement, which he read about online."

"Which one?" he asked.

Cassandra stared. "Which one what?"

"Which brother?"

"Cash." She shoved her hair behind her ears and laughed. "Does it matter? Now your family and your soon-to-be sisters-in-law believe we're engaged. When they started talking about my bare ring finger, I had to excuse myself."

Luke continued to study her for another minute, then he shrugged. "Then we'll find you a ring."

"Just like that? We're going to move to that level?" she asked. "At what point do we stop? Are we going to have to actually get married? Maybe you should suggest a double wedding with Will."

Luke laughed as he took a step toward her and reached for her shoulders. "Take a breath and calm down."

Calm down? How could she? She was still reeling from the realization that at one point in time, Luke had thought about asking her to marry him. Or, he at least had gone to the trouble of getting the ring. Maybe he'd changed his mind or maybe he'd been waiting for a right time that never came—she didn't know. At this point, bringing it up wouldn't solve their issue at hand, and she didn't want to dig back into a host of feelings that had taken a great deal of effort to bury.

"We'll get a ring," Luke told her in that low, slow drawl of his. "We'll pretend to be engaged, but right now the focus will be on Will and Hannah. Maybe we'll flash your hand in a few of our social-media posts, but we don't need to do anything more."

Cassandra shook her head. "I wasn't prepared to be blindsided like that and then when those girls…"

Damn it. She hadn't meant to let that part slip. There was no reason she should let other women bother her. They were faking this relationship because of the women who'd been pestering him. He'd wanted this engagement to deter unwanted attention.

"Don't tell me you were jealous," he said, smirking.

Cassandra tipped up her chin. "That would be ridiculous. I can't be jealous over something that's not even real or a man who isn't even mine."

Those hands slid over her shoulders and the rough pads of his thumbs grazed the side of her neck, then he tipped back her head just slightly as he stepped closer to her.

Cassandra's breath held as her heart beat faster, and nerves curled low in her belly as she waited for him to say something…or to close this gap and kiss her. Not that she *wanted* him to kiss her. There was no need since there was no audience, right?

"You're jealous," he murmured.

"I want you to stay in the role we discussed," she snapped, refusing to let him see just how right he was. "How can we convince people we're in love if you're laughing and chatting it up with other women?"

His lips quirked. "You want to be convincing?"

"We have no choice."

"Sorry."

"What?"

He didn't say another word before his mouth descended onto her lips…and that's when she realized he'd used her code word. Cassandra's knees weakened and she gripped his wrists to hold herself up.

Damn him for still being able to make her weak in the knees.

Luke claimed her with a powerful kiss and everything about him was so familiar, yet so new. How could this be the same man she loved so long ago? Now he was so much more—sexier, bolder and much more in control than she remembered.

Before she could stop herself—a theme with her as of late—Cassandra wrapped her arms around his waist and aligned their hips. She wanted to feel him, all of him. If he was going to be so demanding with this kiss, then so was she. There was a fire burning inside her. As clichéd and silly as that sounded, she didn't know another way to describe what she was feeling. She was hot…too hot. She needed something more—she needed Luke.

Maybe coming back had been a mistake, but she was here now and would have to face her past *and* present feelings at some point.

He released her face and gripped her hips as he spun her around. Cassandra found herself being lifted and then set down onto something sturdy— a desk, maybe?

Luke settled between her spread knees and she arched against his touch. When he nipped at her bottom lip and broke the kiss, she stared up at him as she tried to catch her breath.

"What are we doing?" he muttered, gazing down with hunger in his eyes.

"Ignoring the red flags," she panted.

"This isn't right." But he didn't step back. "Why is this wrong when it feels too damn good?"

Cassandra braced her hands behind her as she watched various complex emotions play over his face.

"This was never our problem, Luke. Sex with you was the easy part."

He laughed. "Easy. Hell, honey, none of this is easy."

Cassandra closed her eyes and tried to focus on calming her breathing and her nerves. No matter how much she wanted him, having an intimate re-

lationship right now would just mess things up…
and not only her business, but also her heart.

Cassandra eased off the desk, causing Luke to
take another step back. He continued to study her
and she could tell by that familiar look in his eyes
that he was turned on and just as ravenous for her
as she was for him.

But…she'd been right. Sex had always been the
easy part of their relationship. Communication had
been their downfall—clearly, considering she'd
just found out tonight he'd had an engagement ring
for her eight years ago.

"We need to figure out what we're telling your
family," Cassandra repeated. "If you want to pretend
with them, fine. If you want to tell them the truth,
that's fine. But we need to be on the same page."

Luke raked a hand through his messy hair and
sighed. "I can't lie to them. I wouldn't do that and
I wouldn't ask you to. I know how close you were
with them once."

From the moment Cassandra had met Luke,
she'd thought of Gavin, Will, and Cash as the
brothers she'd never had. She'd grown up an only
child with a single father. He'd been her only family, and when he passed away after a stroke when
she'd been only twenty-three, she'd instantly taken
even more to the Sutherlands. Travis and Dana
had welcomed her with open arms and treated her
like the daughter they'd never had. Losing them

had been another blow when she'd left town. She hadn't just left Luke—she'd left her second family.

Starting over hadn't been easy and it hadn't been fast, but she'd made a life for herself in Lexington. That was yet another reason why she couldn't get wrapped up with Luke now. There was no way in hell she could go back to what it had been like at that point in time. She wasn't so sure she could recover from another broken heart.

"I'll tell them tonight once we close," Luke decided. "Do you want to hang around? No touching, no kissing. Just hang around here for a while."

Cassandra tipped up her head. "Why?"

He shrugged again in that casual manner he always had. Sometimes she couldn't tell if he really didn't care, or if he just kept his emotions guarded.

"Because I like having you here," he finally admitted. "It's nice having you back in town and we can at least be friendly after everything, right?"

Friends. Sure. That sounded logical, didn't it?

Then again, she'd never kissed her friends like that and she sure as hell had never wanted to rip off her friends' clothes.

"I'll stay," she told him with a smile. "So long as you buy my drinks."

Luke's quirky grin widened. "Anything you want."

And that was the most loaded statement she'd heard since she hit Beaumont Bay.

Six

"You're a damn fool."

Will's outburst was no surprise to Luke. All of the brothers had been taken with Cassandra from the beginning, years ago. They'd all been stunned when she had left town and fully blamed Luke. They'd said he was so wrapped up in his business that he'd let her go without a fight. He'd told them at the time that if she wanted to go, then she wasn't the woman for him. If she could walk away so easily, then they weren't meant to be. Why should he have to choose between the personal and the professional? At the time, he'd thought he could have both.

And that's how he'd ended up alone, with the most successful bars in Tennessee.

Now that Luke had explained the current deal he and Cassandra had set up, all of his brothers glared at him. Gavin relaxed back on one of the sofas, Will leaned against the railing and Cash sat on a high stool nursing a beer. All sets of eyes were directly on Luke and he wished he would've sent this news out in a text instead of waiting for the bar to close to tell them in person.

"What did you expect me to do?" he asked, defending himself. "Cassandra needed help and so did I. It was a perfect setup."

"You think I wouldn't have given Cassandra a chance to talk with Hannah?" Will asked. "It would have all worked out without you going to such extremes and practically blackmailing her."

Luke couldn't have been so sure, and he'd needed Cassandra to play his devoted girlfriend. So far, the ruse was working and social media was exploding with "Lassandra" hashtags and posts. And with a few exceptions, women were now leaving him alone.

But he hadn't blackmailed Cassandra into anything. She could have turned him down and walked away. They were both using each other to get what they wanted and that's what was called a win-win.

"So how long are you two planning on playing this charade?" Cash asked.

Luke sighed. "Until Will's wedding. We'll go our separate ways then."

"Just like that?" Gavin chimed in with a disapproving grunt. "That seems cold. I mean, I'm a lawyer and that's even heartless to me."

Cold and heartless, those were the very last things Luke felt when it came to Cassandra. And he was positive once Will's wedding rolled around in just under two months, he and Cassandra would be more than ready to get back to their own lives.

"Do you feel nothing seeing her again after all this time?" Will asked. "I can't imagine losing Hannah and then seeing her again years later and trying to pretend like everything is normal. She's not some old classmate, Luke. She was the woman you wanted to spend your life with at one time."

"We're two different people now," Luke argued. He shook his head and got to his feet. "Listen, Cassandra and I have this under control. Okay? I just didn't want to lie to you guys, but you have to keep up the charade."

"Do you think this is fair to Cassandra?"

Luke turned to Cash and glared. "Are you being serious right now? She came to me and needed my help."

"You could've helped her without asking for something in return," Cash claimed.

Luke raked a hand through his hair and seriously wished like hell he would've just texted this whole thing and then he could've ignored their opinions.

"It's done now and I just need you guys to go along with this until after Will's wedding. Is that asking too much?"

His brothers continued to stare at him with their judgmental gazes. Luke was tired from the late hours he'd been keeping. He'd been staying until close for the last couple of weeks because there were so many new artists performing and he wanted to be there to support the folks he had booked. He always wanted them to feel welcome in his establishment.

But even when he was home, Luke's thoughts kept turning to Cassandra. He couldn't help but relive their time together from years ago and compare that woman to the woman he knew now. There were certainly similarities, but there were also some changes he couldn't help but hone in on.

Her determination, the strong will, that sassy walk, and her quick wit—maybe all of those things came with life experience, or maybe she'd been that amazing all along. Maybe he'd been so wrapped up in his own world that he'd totally missed the fact that he wasn't even trying to combine business and pleasure until it was too late.

"I'll go along with this ridiculous charade, but if you hurt Cassandra again—"

"Wait," Luke said, cutting off Gavin. "What do you mean if I hurt Cassandra again? She's the one who left the first time."

"Because you were putting her behind everything else in your life," Gavin retorted. "I can't believe she waited as long as she did before giving up on you."

Luke rarely got pissed with his brothers, but right now he didn't like how they were Team Cassandra and not seeing his point of view at all here.

"I'm not asking for opinions, I'm only asking that you keep the secret."

He met each of his brothers' gazes until they all nodded in agreement. Luke hated feeling like he'd just been put through a mental battle that he wasn't quite sure he'd won. Now that he'd talked to his brothers, he needed to have a conversation with his parents, and that was going to be equally as enjoyable.

"I'm heading home," he told them. "Be sure to take the service elevator when you leave. I'll come in early tomorrow and clean up whatever mess you heathens have made."

Without waiting for a reply, Luke excused himself and headed toward his private elevator. Every part of him wanted to stop off at the penthouse, but normal people were likely sleeping right now.

Odd that his first reaction when he was troubled was wanting to reach for Cassandra. That had been the case at one time in his life, but not now. She was nothing more than the one who got away and the one who was now his temporary, very fake fiancée.

"What do you think?"

Cassandra glanced at the spread of floral options and sketches and could tell by Hannah's exasperated tone that she was confused. Knowing when it was time to take a little control out of the bride's hands, Cassandra pulled her three favorites for the venue and slid the others to the side.

"Okay, so I'm going to give you my own personal opinion," Cassandra began. "And I'm only doing this because from what we've chosen so far, I'm confident I know your tastes."

After two weeks of working diligently on the wedding, Hannah had also been recording her new album and doing interviews, which had taken her out of town for a few days. So when she was home, Cassandra had to take every moment she could and yet still make their meetings seem like a zero-stress environment.

"I trust your judgment," Hannah stated. "In fact, I'd love to take the pressure off me for just a moment and talk about you."

"Me?"

Hannah's smile widened. "Yes. I'm aware that you and Luke used to be involved and Will told me the other evening that you two are engaged, but not really engaged."

Cringing, Cassandra nodded. "It's complicated."

Hannah got to her feet, then walked over to the wet bar in the corner of her sitting room and grabbed two glasses. After pouring mimosas, Hannah came back over to the sofa and handed one of the glasses to Cassandra.

"Thank you." Cassandra smiled and took the drink. "I'm not sure this will even help at this point."

"So I'm just trying to understand." Hannah took a sip and eased back into her seat. "And, please, tell me if I overstep here."

Cassandra couldn't help but laugh. "I'm planning the wedding of my favorite singer and I'm in her house and she wants to offer advice. I promise— you're not overstepping."

Hannah laughed, too. "Well, thank you, but I'm just a regular person with honest feelings. Which makes me wonder how you're dealing with all of this. From what Will told me, you and Luke ended things a long time ago. But still, is this all weird or are you okay?"

Nobody had asked her about her feelings on this bizarre setup. And, honestly, Cassandra hadn't even taken the time to think of them herself. She'd gotten wrapped up in this whirlwind of a dream job, then a fake engagement, and now being splashed all over social media as "Lassandra." All in a few weeks' time.

"I'm fine," Cassandra assured Hannah. "It's strange being back here with Luke, but familiar at the same time, if that makes sense."

"If you don't mind my asking, what happened the first time? I mean, you are an amazing woman and Luke is such a great guy."

Cassandra took a moment to gather her thoughts as she took a sip of her mimosa. "Luke is a great guy, but we just weren't great together. Well, we were…until the day we weren't. Does that make any sense?"

Hannah pursed her lips. "About as much sense as the fake engagement."

"Pretty much." Cassandra sighed and glanced down to the stack of three options for the floral arrangements. "Okay, let's circle back to your wedding. Fall is such a gorgeous time in Tennessee, so I really don't think you can go wrong with any of these options."

Cassandra splayed them all out onto the glass table in front of the sofa and waited while Hannah glanced over each one.

"They're all so perfect," Hannah muttered. "I feel like Hallie should be here to help me decide. Sometimes she knows what I like before I do."

"I imagine that's just one of the perks of having a twin."

Hannah nodded. "There are many, that's for sure. But, since she's not here, tell me which one you would choose."

"It's not my wedding."

Hannah shrugged. "Pretend it is. What would you choose if you were me?"

Even though she loved them all, Cassandra pointed to the images of the greenery with varieties of white blooms.

"This one," she told Hannah. "I love the simplicity, especially with it being an outdoor wedding. Around the lake and being in the fall, I think the delicate green and white will be timeless. Plus, it will carry over so nicely to the reception at The Cheshire and the decor Luke already has in place."

"And do you love the idea of the lakeside gazebo ceremony?" Hannah asked.

Cassandra smiled and nodded. "I've always wanted an outdoor fall wedding. When I get to plan those, it's like a little piece of me gets even more excited. I treat all my brides equally, but this time of year and especially being by the lake surrounded by colorful mountains… Well, this is just going to be absolutely breathtaking."

Cassandra stared down at the graphic and sighed. "The way the greenery is draped around the posts and the cream flowers are intermingled, and then the sprays nestled around the base of the stage…it's just so romantic and dreamy. I can see the bridesmaids in their dusty pink, holding their tight bouquets of cream buds and greenery sprays, the taupe chair covers all adorned with a simple floral arrangement on each one, the cream-colored petals sprinkled down the aisle between the VIP guests."

"You make things sound so perfect," Hannah stated. "I think you've talked me in to this one."

Cassandra blinked and glanced at the option she'd just described. "Are you positive? This is your wedding, not mine."

"You'll be planning yours soon enough," Hannah replied with a smile.

A little stunned at the statement, Cassandra shook her head. "Oh, I'm not so sure about that. I think I'd have to have a man in my life before I'd be ready to choose between lilies or hydrangea."

"You have a man in your life." Hannah patted Cassandra's knee and grinned. "You may be pretending, but who knows. Maybe the old sparks are still there?"

If by sparks she meant sexual attraction, that was a definite yes. Who knew how things would be between them now? She could only assume the sex would still be great, if not greater than it had been before.

Damn it. She'd tried not to let her mind go there,

but now she couldn't help herself. Intimacy with Luke had been off the charts. He'd always known just how to touch her, exactly how to make her feel amazing. He'd been such a giving lover and their intimacy was something she'd never been able to find with anyone else since…and she'd tried. Mercy she'd tried, but all that her trying had done was lead to dreams that involved Luke in a very erotic manner that only left her satisfied in her sleep. Which was something she'd never admit to anyone, ever.

"You're smiling."

Hannah's statement pulled Cassandra from her fantasy as it was just starting to get out of control. And, damn it, she hadn't realized she'd been smiling.

"Maybe there's something left over after all?" Hannah asked with a teasing grin. She took a sip of her mimosa then set the glass on the table. "Teasing aside, if there's something you want, maybe you should go after it. I know Will and I danced around each other because we didn't think being together was right for our careers, but there's so much more than what brings in a paycheck. Had we only focused on that, all of this that is so real between us could have been lost. We have to take charge of our own happiness sometimes instead of waiting for someone else to give it to us."

As much as Cassandra loved getting advice from Hannah, and this was solid, sound advice, things just weren't going to magically turn from pretend to real. They'd had their chance once and now they were both happy in their lives and their careers. They'd made their own paths and just because they'd been thrust into a situation that kept bringing up their past didn't mean they had to pick up where they'd left off.

Besides, he'd had his opportunity and he'd blown it. Luke had chosen his business ventures over her. Why shouldn't she chase her own dreams and be successful? She'd taken time to build and grow her career, create a foundation for herself in the wedding industry, and she wasn't about to let Luke derail her now that she was branching out on her own and making a name for herself.

"I think you've got too much wedding and floating hearts on your mind," Cassandra joked. "Let's focus on your love life. It's less complicated."

"Love doesn't have to be complicated," Hannah replied, then laughed. "I think that's in one of my songs."

Yeah, well, songs and real life didn't always go hand-in-hand. Cassandra was truly happy with where she was on her journey. She didn't need love or a man to complete her. Fulfilling other people's happily-ever-after dreams was more than enough for her.

So why did she have a yawning ache in her chest that told her she was only lying to herself?

Seven

Luke glanced again at the headline on the social-media page and he still couldn't pinpoint his emotions.

Another Sutherland Brother to be Married

He leaned back in his leather desk chair and sighed. Luke didn't want to be married, not now or ever. At one time, back when Cass was in his life the first time, he'd been working toward asking her. He'd been laying a firm foundation for their lives, but she'd seen that as him pushing her aside and putting his work first. She'd crushed his soul when she'd left without seeing that everything he did was for her.

He'd never let himself get that attached to anyone ever again and he wasn't in any need for such nonsense now, either.

The glaring headline was like a sucker punch to the gut. This particular article had a photo of him and Cassandra, one that she'd posted on her social-media account just this morning. She'd taken the selfie a few days ago when she'd popped into the bar. It was a quick picture of him kissing her on the cheek, her smile wide and quite convincing. No sooner had the photo been taken than she'd rushed back out the door to do more wedding planning.

And maybe that's what irked him. The way this arrangement seemed like a business deal rather than... What? This *was* a business deal. They had nothing else between them other than this agreed-upon charade, which was precisely the way he wanted things.

So why did he still get an unsettling ache inside each time he saw something new in the press?

He clicked on another article about them and cringed at the headline on this one.

Another Sutherland Engaged...but Where's the Ring?

The piece went on to joke that maybe he was giving Cassandra one of his bars instead of the gift of a rock on her hand. This wasn't the first time a ring had been hinted at, and honestly, after a few weeks of this game he really should've gotten her one.

But thinking of getting her a ring only brought back the memory of the time he actually had bought a ring. He'd scraped his own money together to buy something he thought she'd love. He'd been working on getting two of his bars up and open and he'd wanted to do it all on his own with the wise investments he'd made and a few loans.

He still had that damn ring. When she'd left, he hadn't been in the mindset to do anything with it, then when he'd attempted to get back to his life and start again without her, he hadn't wanted to return it. When he'd asked his mother for help choosing the ring, Luke had no clue when he would eventually give it to Cassandra. He wasn't ready then, but he assumed the day would come when they'd get married. The timing had never felt just right and then she was gone.

For reasons he couldn't explain, he'd hung on to the piece as some crazy symbol of what he'd let slip away. Every time he saw the velvet box in his safe, he was reminded of how far he'd come, that if he wanted something, to go for it.

So many thoughts swirled around in his head and before he could talk himself out of this terrible idea, he opened his messages and sent one to Cassandra. He held his breath waiting for her reply, but once it arrived, Luke got to his feet. He'd put a plan into motion and now he would have to see how it all played out.

Cassandra stepped off the private elevator of The Cheshire and scanned the crowd. Another night with a packed house of VIP guests and many from the high society of Beaumont Bay. People were laughing, drinking and chatting, and the band was getting set up. Cassandra noted the band tonight was made up of two young women who looked nervous yet excited. They kept smiling at each other as they stood just off the stage. Luke came into view as he approached them. Cassandra eased a little closer and overheard him giving them a speech.

"You guys will be fine," he told them. "I wouldn't have invited you here if I didn't think you were awesome. You both need a boost of confidence and this is where you'll get it. You know I only have the best artists on my stage."

"That's why we're so nervous," one of the girls laughed. "But thank you. This has been one of our dreams, to play The Cheshire stage."

"Once people hear you, you guys will be booked solid and I'll be begging to get back on your busy schedule," Luke stated. "The crowd is ready. Are you guys?"

The girls glanced at each other and nodded.

"I'll go introduce you," he said.

Cassandra moved to the bar as Luke took the stage. As always, the moment he grabbed the mic, the crowd started cheering. Luke Sutherland was a natural charmer and he could hold anyone captive… and she was no exception.

He'd texted her earlier and asked her to come up this evening because there was another impressive new band and because he had something to show her. Intrigued by his message, she'd agreed. Then she'd had a hell of a time trying to get her focus back on Hannah's wedding.

Between Hannah being gushy with her ideas about love yesterday during their meeting and then Luke texting her tonight, Cassandra's thoughts were all over the place. Not to mention that she had weddings she was working on remotely, and was planning ahead for the brides who had come to her looking to book for a year or more out. Cassandra's stress level was higher than she'd ever let it get before.

She wished she could just jump straight to the end of this journey and go back to her life in Lexington. Her new business would surely take off and she could focus on that and future brides instead of Luke.

"Gin and tonic with extra lime?"

Cassandra turned to the bartender—Miles, she believed his name was—and smiled.

"You remembered."

"That's part of the job," he replied. "But I also couldn't forget the future Mrs. Sutherland's order."

Future Mrs. Sutherland...that would be her. Well, it *would* be her, if all of this was real.

The lump in her throat stopped Cassandra from saying anything else. She hadn't thought of herself as the future Mrs. Sutherland in a long, long time. Not since she'd had the naive notion that she might actually hold that title one day.

"Here you go," Miles stated as he slid her drink across the bar top on a leather coaster imprinted with the bar logo. "Let me know if I can get you anything else."

He moved on to the next customer as Cassandra nodded her thanks and picked up her tumbler.

"Glad you could make it."

She jumped and turned to see Luke right behind her. The band started up, playing something fast and peppy, getting the crowd excited. The drumbeat seemed to match the rhythm of her heart.

"You intrigued me," she admitted, then took a sip of her drink.

"Extra lime?" he asked, nodding to her glass.

"You have a good memory."

His gaze ran over her face, and he seemed to be

studying her or trying to gauge what to say next. The rooftop bar might be packed, but she didn't notice anyone else except for Luke. He took a step closer and reached up to smooth a strand of hair away from her cheek. He took a little extra time in trailing a fingertip along her jaw.

"Come to my office."

He hadn't exactly whispered, since the area was too loud, but he didn't shout, which made the command seem intimate. Cassandra nodded and when he reached for her, she held her breath.

Luke's arm slid around her waist as he led her behind the bar and to the private hallway to his office. The door slid open and then closed as they stepped in. Once they were alone, the music was drowned out, and Cassandra was glad she held her drink so her hands had something to do.

Why was she so nervous? Or was it not nervousness, but…arousal?

She was such a mess, she couldn't even figure out her own thoughts right now. After a quick sip, she moved farther into the office and leaned against the edge of a leather club chair.

"So what is this mystery you called me up here for?"

Still standing across the room, Luke sighed and crossed his arms over his chest. His eyes remained locked on hers and a muscle ticked in his jaw.

"It's come to my attention that you still don't have a ring," he began. "We need to fix that."

Confused, Cassandra shook her head. "I thought we discussed just telling everyone we were going to choose one later."

"Considering we've been engaged for a few weeks now, I'd say that's long enough."

Luke walked to his desk and opened the drawer. Cassandra turned to face him and watched as he pulled out a velvet box.

"Luke, I don't think—"

His eyes met hers. "You will wear a ring. My ring."

He circled back around the desk and came to stand before her. When he lifted the lid, Cassandra gasped at the simple gold band with a pearl in the middle, encircled by tiny diamonds.

"I remembered you used to always wear this little pair of pearl earrings so I wanted to get something that you'd like," he told her. "I saw this and thought it suited you."

She stared at the stunning ring for another moment before looking back up to him. Had he actually gone somewhere and picked out this ring for her, or was this the original ring she'd heard about from his brothers? There was so much to interpret in this moment and Cassandra was terrified to delve deeper into all the questions she had. She was even more afraid of what the answers would be.

"I can't… This is… Luke…"

"I'm glad you're speechless," he laughed. "That means you like it."

She continued to stare, unsure of what to say or what to do. She hadn't wanted him to present her with a ring—that would make all of this a little too real. Even though years had passed since she'd dreamed of this moment with him, having him give her a ring now only thrust her mentally back to a time she'd tried to forget.

"I don't think this is a good idea," she insisted.

Luke reached for her drink and set it on his desk, then turned back and that damn ring glinted in the light. It was so beautiful, yet simple, and something she would have chosen herself. He'd done such a beautiful job and she still had those pearl earrings he'd mentioned.

"When did you go get a ring, anyway?" she asked.

"That's not important and this *is* a good idea," he countered. "We're playing the role of being engaged and I don't half-ass anything."

When he slid the ring from the slot in the box, she held her breath. Luke pocketed the box before reaching for her hand. Without a word, without getting down on one knee, without any fanfare or romantic gestures one should have with an engagement, he eased the ring onto her finger.

Definitely not how she'd thought her engagement would go. The ring felt so foreign, nearly as much as this crazy gesture. There was something almost cold and sterile about this moment. A shiver crept through her and she couldn't suppress it.

"You okay?"

Cassandra continued to stare at the ring on her finger and felt the burn in her throat. Emotions were welling up, yet she couldn't afford to cry now. Never in her life had she thought she'd get upset when a man put a ring on her finger, but…well, this wasn't exactly the moment she had dreamed of her whole life.

She was in the business of romance and milestones, memorable moments. She rejoiced in happy couples and shared their wedding journeys with them. Yet she couldn't even be excited about her own moment because nothing was real…except that shattered heart she'd thought she'd mended.

"Fine," she lied, taking her gaze off the ring and putting it back onto her official fake fiancé. "But at the end of all this you will get the ring back."

"If that's what you want."

"It is," she commanded. There was no way she wanted any type of souvenir from her time here in Beaumont Bay unless it was a favor from Will and Hannah's wedding.

"We really should have done this before now," Luke told her. "We can play it off by saying that we didn't want to overshadow Cash's or Will's engagements. We should definitely post more photos, but we shouldn't be obvious about it. Let the media draw their own conclusions and keep the mystery behind the ring."

The ring. Something so small and simple, yet it held so much importance in her life right now. Why couldn't he have gotten her something big and gaudy? Something flashy for the world to see from a distance?

No, he'd gotten her something delicate and soft, something that truly summed up her style, a piece she would be sorry to give back. Because just like their arrangement, this engagement, and the ring, would all vanish in a short time.

"Whatever you want," she murmured.

Luke stepped forward, closing the gap between them. He took her left hand in his and held it up, but his eyes remained on hers.

"This is what we agreed on," he murmured. "You're mine."

"For now."

"For now," he agreed.

He tugged her gently until she fell against his chest and he released her hand to wrap his arm behind her back. Cassandra's hands flattened against his chest. The warm scent of his cologne wafted around her. The strength of his body aroused her even more. The familiarity was present, but there was still something about him that was new, thrilling, exciting. She wanted more, even though she shouldn't because he clearly still wasn't ready for any commitment. Hell, he'd been voted the most eligible bachelor and had women flocking around him and he wasn't interested. He was still just as married to his job as he'd ever been...possibly more.

"What are you doing?"

"What we both want. And I'm not apologizing."

He leaned in closer and Cassandra eased back her head slightly. "Is this a bad idea?"

"Maybe," he allowed. "But we still both want the same thing."

"We shouldn't want more," she murmured, but there was no conviction in her tone and she knew as well as he did that her words were in vain. "Desire isn't something I can fight. It never has been with you."

And maybe having him put that damn ring on her finger had her thoughts a little more jumbled than usual, because she was actually considering letting him do whatever he wanted—what she wanted.

"I don't want to fight," he told her. "I'm just tired of pretending I don't want you."

He wanted her.

She'd known, but hearing the words said aloud had even more knots forming in her stomach. Maybe coming back here had been a mistake. Maybe she should've contacted Will directly and simply asked about being his wedding planner.

But no. She'd come straight to the one man she should have kept her distance from. After all these years, though, she thought she'd be fine seeing him again. She thought they'd put enough of a gap between them that the past wouldn't interfere with her future plans.

She'd been wrong.

"This isn't a real relationship," she explained. "We can't complicate things with…"

"Sex."

There it was. The word they'd danced around for a while, and now it was out in the open and hovering between them.

"Why can't we?" he asked, his mouth hovering just a breath from hers. "Are you going to tell me you don't wonder if we're even better than we were? Are you going to tell me you don't want this just as much as I do?"

She needed distance. She couldn't think with him touching her, not with that strength he possessed and that heavy-lidded stare he owned.

Cassandra eased from his embrace and took a few steps away, taking in a deep breath to calm her shaky nerves and get control over herself.

"My wants are irrelevant," she stated when she turned back to face him. "And so are yours for that matter."

Luke continued to stare at her, and it was the silence between them that had her questioning herself yet again. Why wasn't she taking what he offered? He'd been right in saying they both wanted this. She couldn't even lie to herself, let alone him, because she did want him. Part of her wondered if they'd be even better than before, while the other part wondered if she'd get lost in the lust and passion and forget that this was all a fake, temporary relationship.

"I should go," she told him.

"You don't want to."

Cassandra shrugged—there was reason not to be honest. "Like I said, that doesn't matter. I didn't come here for a fling and that's all this would be. I have no room in my life for anything more."

At least not with the man who'd shattered her heart years ago.

Luke said nothing and Cassandra couldn't take the tension, or the desire emanating from him, for another second. She went to the door and tapped the security panel to slide open the wall. Immediately, the blaring music surrounded her. Happy customers were all still milling about while singing along and drinking. Everyone continued on about their lives as if hers hadn't just taken a drastic turn.

How was she going to get through the next few weeks before the wedding? She would have to stay busy. She would have to focus on work and not the fact that she still wanted the hell out of her ex-lover turned fake fiancé.

He'd wanted a fling and she couldn't deny she wanted him, too. But at what cost? Because no matter how much they enjoyed themselves, even that small bit of happiness would be ripped away in the end, and Cassandra didn't want any more heartache where Luke was concerned.

Eight

Luke called himself all kinds of a fool for the way he'd treated Cassandra. She deserved better than his pushy assumptions and now he had to do something to make up for his actions.

He hadn't seen or spoken to her in a few days and he knew from talking with Will that Cassandra and Hannah were busy planning all things wedding. She was here for a job, not to be harassed by him. She'd come to him for help and he'd turned the tables on her by asking for something of his own. He'd wanted to prove to himself that he could be close to her and be completely unaffected. Then he'd wondered if he should take advantage of this prime opportunity for a little payback.

But that was a jerk move. How could he be cruel when Cass's leaving long ago had obviously been the best thing for both of them? They were now successful in their own ways and had built happy lives, right?

Yeah, he owed her a damn big apology and he was going to do that right now. He shot off a quick text that he had a surprise for her and he would pick her up at noon.

Luke rested his arms on the railing of his balcony off his master suite and stared at his cell screen. Immediately, he saw she was typing a response. He thought for sure she would tell him no, or to go to hell…both of which he deserved.

I'm busy right now. Make it one.

That extra hour was even better. Now Luke could plan appropriately. His mind traveled back to the twentysomething guy he'd once been who'd wanted to give her the world. So much had changed in both of their lives and he found there was still a sliver of him that missed what they used to share. Not just the intimacy, but their friendship. He hadn't even realized how much of a void her leaving had left until she'd returned.

Luke pushed off the railing and pocketed his

phone. He'd made sure to let the managers of his bars know exactly where he'd be today in case of an emergency, but he had such competent employees, he didn't worry one bit. They could certainly all manage without him for one day.

He didn't recall the last time he'd taken an entire day off, but if anything warranted some time away, Cassandra sure as hell did.

With a little burst of hope and excitement, Luke put his plan in motion and started counting down the hours until he could see Cassandra again.

With a quick click of her mouse, Cassandra sent the rush order to the florist for all of the fresh blooms the local florist would need to create a masterpiece for Hannah and Will's perfect day.

The penthouse echoed with the buzz at her door. She got up from where she was sitting at the corner desk and smoothed a hand down her pants. She'd been told to wear pants and boots, and to be comfortable. Now she was intrigued, and wondered if they were going hiking or if there was something else on Luke's mind that she didn't know about. He'd been cryptic with his texts when she tried to get him to tell her what was going on.

Cassandra blew out a breath and headed toward the door. She would have to face him at some time, and if they were going out, that was the best option. Staying in or being alone with him wouldn't be smart at this point. She'd been dreaming of him these last few nights and all that did was leave her aching and wanting.

She had to shove aside all of that nonsense and focus on the job. There was no reason she couldn't be friendly, though, right?

Cassandra flicked the lock on the door and opened it to reveal Luke standing there holding a large gift bag.

With a laugh, Cassandra eased back to let him inside. "It's not my birthday, so what's the bag all about?"

Luke stepped into the penthouse and set down the bag at her feet. He stood straight up and pointed to the tissue-filled gift.

"I wanted to bring you something to start off my apology, but flowers are overrated and I had no clue what to do." He let out a laugh and raked a hand over the afternoon scruff on his jawline. "I figure you're a wedding planner, so a planner would be useful. Then the lady at the store said you can't have a planner without special markers, then she showed me this whole display of sticker things on a wall."

Cassandra watched as he fumbled over his words and sought some attempt at an apology. She crossed her arms and simply waited for him to finish.

"So I had no clue what the hell you had or didn't

have, so I just told the lady to give me everything from that wall of stickers. Well, I didn't have her give me the baby or expecting-mother packs because, well…for obvious reasons."

Cassandra didn't know whether to hug him for being so damn adorable, or inform him that planners and stickers weren't quite the type of planning she did for a career.

But she absolutely loved the gift. She loved the gesture. She really hadn't expected anything so sweet from him. Not only had he done something thoughtful, but he'd also shown his vulnerable side. Never once in all the time she'd known him had she ever seen Luke admit he didn't know something, or venture into a territory that wasn't in his wheelhouse. The fact that he'd gone into a store and stepped outside his obvious comfort zone all to show he was sorry…

And other than that one kiss, he'd never told her he was sorry for anything. Who was this new Luke and why was he being so damn perfect? She didn't want to find him even more charming and adorable than usual. She could handle the sexy Luke, but the tender side… She wasn't so sure what to do with that.

Cassandra bent down, pulled out the tissue paper and laughed at the sight of what was inside. "You really did go all out, didn't you?"

"Considering I was a jerk the other night for

propositioning you into a fake engagement..." He raked a hand over his hair and sighed. "I know you wanted marriage when we were together before, so that wasn't fair."

Cassandra stood straight up and met his gaze. There was something there beyond the apology she could clearly see. It was that other emotion she couldn't quite put a label on.

"No, it wasn't," she agreed. "But this is where we are now."

"I can't help but think there's something to explore here."

His statement shocked her and immediately her heart kicked up. "What?" she whispered.

With a shrug, he took a slight step forward. "I don't know, Cass. I just can't help but feel that pull. It's strong, it's completely physical, but it's there and damn difficult to ignore."

In addition to that fast heartbeat, now she had a quiver of nerves curling in her belly. She'd obviously had those same feelings since she'd come back to Beaumont Bay, but now that they were out in the open, she didn't know what to say.

"I'm not trying to make you uncomfortable," he added. "And I don't know what the hell I want, but you deserved an apology and I plan on making it up to you."

Then Luke gestured toward the door, and suddenly, the moment was gone. "Ready to go?" he asked.

Just like that, he'd swept in here with the most adorable gift, given her a heartfelt apology, and admitted he wanted to explore something more. Damn if she wasn't in trouble here and she had no way out. The only way to go was forward and she hoped she didn't get crushed in the process.

Cassandra pushed aside her fears because there was nothing she could do about them now. "Are you going to give me a hint as to what we're doing?"

"Not one."

She couldn't help but laugh as she went to get her purse.

"You won't need that," he told her.

She froze and glanced over her shoulder. "No? Now I'm really intrigued."

Cassandra grabbed her room key from her purse and slid it into her back pocket. Nerves curled through her belly at the anticipation of what Luke had in mind. This was the Luke she remembered—always doing sweet things. Granted, the passionate Luke from the other night was also familiar and damn difficult to turn away.

He'd admitted he wanted something physical. Could it really be that simple between them? After all the drama they'd been through, she really didn't know.

But they did have a deal between them and she

planned to hold up her end. A few more pictures on social media to keep this farce going wouldn't hurt. Which reminded her to also grab her cell.

"I'm ready," she told him after she'd gotten her phone. "Should we do a selfie now or is there something more exhilarating that will be a better backdrop than my hotel living room?"

Luke smiled, and damn it, he was irresistible... yet somehow she'd resisted him. She'd pushed him away, but since then, their attraction and sexual tension was all she'd thought of.

Cassandra wanted to rewind to the other night and just let go. What would have happened if she'd shoved aside those red flags waving around inside her head? Where would they be now if they'd just let this fling happen? They were adults; they weren't the naive couple they used to be. Her eyes were wide open now...and she wasn't sure she could keep resisting him.

"I have something more exciting planned," he assured her. "Unless you want a quick kiss selfie?"

He waggled his eyebrows at her, still with that naughty smile in place. Cassandra crossed to him and smacked his chest.

"Nice try," she told him. "I'll wait to see what you have planned."

"Does that mean no kiss?" he joked.

"Not right now. I'd like to see what you have in

store and how we can spin it to our social media. That is the whole reason for this date, I assume?"

Luke's smile faltered slightly. "When I planned this, I hadn't given social media or other women a single thought. I just wanted to take a breather from everything and I figured you needed a break, too. And I wanted to see you smile."

Oh, hell. When he said things like that, she couldn't remember why she was ignoring her own desires. The man wasn't just sexy and successful— he was kind and generous…and he clearly wanted her.

She had to get out of here or she would forget all the reasons she couldn't get entangled with Luke Sutherland again. The bomb his brothers had dropped about Luke having a ring for her years ago had taken root in her mind and she thought about it every time her gaze caught the current band on her finger. Layer all of that information with her current emotions and she was a walking wreck.

"Everything okay?"

Luke's question pulled her back to the present and Cassandra pasted on a smile. "Perfectly fine. I'm ready for more of my surprise. You know I love them."

She bent down and slid the tissue paper back inside the gift bag, then took the heavy bag to the small dining table just off the living room. She still couldn't believe he'd done all of that for her.

Just that gesture alone had her heart softening. She couldn't imagine how she'd feel at the end of this day. Maybe she would completely succumb to his charms and her needs.

Nine

Luke hadn't known what Cassandra's reaction would be, but he smiled when he saw her face light up as he turned onto the lane that led to his barn and pasture. He'd called ahead and had his stable hand get two of the stallions ready.

"Who owns all of this?" Cassandra asked as she looked out onto the fields lined with white fencing and horses dotting the horizon.

"I do."

Her attention jerked to him. "You own all this land?"

Luke pulled up to the stable and killed the engine, then turned to face her. Her shocked expression had him laughing and swelling with pride.

"Did you think I just tended bar and partied all day and night?"

Cassandra stared for a moment before shrugging and turning back to the acreage. "I never thought about it. I mean, I just assumed if you owned all of those businesses, then you were married to those. How do you have time to come out here?"

"It's just like anything else. I make time. And as much as I love my bars and all the people I meet, there are times when I need to get away."

That was something that had changed since she'd left. He'd never made time for anything else other than work before that point. But he'd learned the benefit of taking a break, and now, he was taking time for her. Their outing had nothing to do with the fake relationship. There was no one around to care or see.

Cassandra smiled. "You always loved riding."

"If I recall, so did you."

She looked back at him with a sweetness in her smile and a softness in her eyes. "We always said we'd have a horse farm outside Beaumont Bay where we could escape. Looks like you did everything you wanted."

Back then they'd discussed many dreams for the future. But he hadn't been ready to put that ring on her finger and she'd wanted nothing more. He'd gone on to fulfill his every career goal. Wasn't that what he'd wanted? He had the social scene and nightlife in Beaumont Bay, he had his businesses, plus a place to go and decompress when needed.

Clearly they hadn't been on the same page back then. They'd both had dreams, but they'd branched off in different directions. Looking back, maybe that had been the best thing that could have happened to them.

Luke cleared his throat and reached for his door handle. "Let's go have some fun."

She was out of the truck before he could come around and get her door. The late-summer breeze surrounded them, sending her hair dancing around her shoulders. Cassandra lifted her face into the wind and closed her eyes. An instant punch of lust to the gut had him catching his breath. He hadn't thought of the impact bringing her here would have on his mental state. Luke had just wanted to apologize and have a relaxing day.

He hadn't taken into consideration all they'd discussed so long ago. At one time, this was exactly what Cass had dreamed of and what she'd wanted them to share together. He'd always planned on having a place where they could escape from their work and just be alone.

And that's exactly what they were doing now, but definitely not under the circumstances he'd originally envisioned.

Without thinking, Luke reached for her hand

and Cassandra's gaze snapped to his. Now that he was holding her, he didn't want to let go and it had nothing to do with faking this relationship. He couldn't help how he felt. Turning off his desire for her wasn't an option—it never had been.

He curled his fingers around hers and couldn't help but feel an extra lick of lust when she returned the gesture. There was something building here that had absolutely nothing to do with the outside world and nothing to do with their business arrangement.

"I don't remember the last time I went riding," she told him. "This definitely gets you brownie points."

"So I'm forgiven for the other night?" he asked as he led her toward the stable.

"There's nothing to forgive. Things got heated, Luke. It's bound to happen given our history."

Maybe so, but their history had nothing to do with why he felt a pull toward her now. He was intrigued by the woman she'd become and he wanted to learn more. He wanted to know what she'd been doing since she'd left. Maybe he was a masochist for wanting to spend more time with her, for wanting to uncover everything about their time apart. She was only back in town for a short time and Luke wanted to make the most of it.

But he had to remain guarded. She'd been such an intricate part of his world at one time and yet she'd walked away. Getting too emotionally involved now would be such a foolish, naive mistake. He knew better, and quite honestly, he still wasn't looking for anything more than something physical.

"And given the attraction that's still there," she murmured.

Luke's stomach tightened as she tacked on that bold statement. Considering she'd put the brakes on things the other night, he respected her enough to let her take the lead. If she wanted more, then he'd sure as hell give her everything she wanted. But if she only wanted to be friends while she was in town, then that's what he would do, no matter his own desires.

Nobody had ever affected him like Cassandra and now that she was back in town, she had him mesmerized all over again.

He was doomed. That would be the end result of all of this. He might not be in love with her anymore, but that didn't mean he didn't want her. He wanted the hell out of her and the more time he spent with her, the deeper that desire took hold. It threatened to consume him.

As they stepped into the stables, Luke spotted the stallions at the end of the path. Their reins were looped around the hooks and the horses were all set to go. Luke had told his stable hand to make sure everything was set and then make himself scarce. Luke wanted privacy and he wanted Cassandra to enjoy her day without any interruptions.

"They are gorgeous," Cassandra exclaimed as she headed toward the animals. "What are their names?"

"Carl and Stan."

Cassandra laughed. "Those aren't quite the horse names I was imagining. I figured like Thunderbolt, or something strong and powerful."

Luke laughed and reached out to stroke one of the stallions.

"Carl and Stan were two of my regular customers when I first opened The Cheshire. They were best friends who'd been widowed. They came to drink every Thursday night and stayed until I closed. We ended up getting close, as one does with regular customers. They both passed within six months of each other."

"They clearly left an impact on you." Cassandra reached up and slid her hand along Carl's nose. "You're more sentimental than I remember."

Only because he'd become that way after she'd gone. He'd realized what was important in life. When he was left with only his businesses and his dreams, he'd thrown himself into every bit of them to make everything a success. He'd been so close to commitment when he'd lost her—he'd vowed never to lose anything or anyone else again.

"Which one am I riding?" she asked, turning to face him.

"Either one. They're both gentle giants and love to be ridden."

Cassandra unhooked one of the reins and easily slid up into the saddle. "I'll take this guy. I can't wait to see the land. It's so gorgeous from out here. Does it go back far?"

Luke took his own horse and mounted him before easing the reins to turn the stallion. "I own about five hundred acres."

"Five hundred?" she exclaimed. "What are you going to do with all of that property?"

"One day I'll build a house, but I just haven't gotten around to it. I built the stable about five years ago, but I've been too busy to design the house."

Not to mention he couldn't bring himself to zero in on the plans he wanted. It seemed rather silly to build a large house for a party of one. His place now was too big for him. He wasn't looking to marry or start a family, but maybe it would happen for him one day. Hell, he had no idea what his future would look like. He was living in the now and enjoying every minute of the life he'd created.

His mother would love nothing more than for him to catch that marriage bug like Will and Cash, but that just wasn't happening.

When Luke had told his parents about the fake

engagement, his mother had scolded him for multiple reasons, but mainly for not bringing Cassandra around so they could see her.

"Show me around," she told him with a smile.

Luke followed her out into the pasture, wondering if this day would bring more for both of them than just a time to relax.

Hell, what was he thinking?

This day and this fake engagement weren't going to end in some damn fairy tale. Clearly, his brothers' engagements were messing with his head. Luke would do good to remember that Cassandra had walked away once and there wasn't a doubt in his mind she would do it again.

The diamonds on her engagement ring glinted in the sunlight and the pearl seemed to glisten even whiter than before. Cassandra tried to ignore the shimmer and shine as she took in the beauty of Luke's property. All of this seemed so surreal. There were too many elements that were thrusting her back into the past.

At one time this property, and this engagement, would have been real, would have been hers. It would have been her actual life and she would have been living her dream with the perfect man. Would they have children by now? That was one area she hadn't allowed her mind to wander to before, but now that she was seeing all that she had lost, she couldn't help but let her imagination go into that hidden corner she'd kept locked.

But none of that mattered.

No matter how wayward her thoughts were, she couldn't go back in time. And now she was only pretending to have that life she'd once dreamed about. The ring would go back, the fairy-tale romance of riding in open fields would be gone, Luke would go back to his bars and she would go back to her life in Lexington. She'd come to Beaumont Bay only to get the wedding of her career and boost Be My Guest into high-society territory. She'd done that. So why was she wanting more?

"Back here is where I plan on building."

Luke's statement cut into her thoughts and she focused on where he was pointing. There was a slight knoll and just in the distance was a large pond. She could practically picture a stone-and-log home standing tall. Wraparound porches were a must and maybe a second-story balcony off the master. Something masculine and demanding of attention with thick wood beams and dark stone chimneys.

"So you're going to give up living in the Bay?" she asked.

"Eventually. There's a little too much drama in town and I like the peace and quiet this place has to offer."

"Drama? You mean that's still a problem?"

When she'd lived here years ago, there was always something major going on. The place was almost like living in a soap opera. Typically, the emotional chaos revolved around Mags Dumond—self-dubbed First Lady of Beaumont Bay. Even though her husband, the mayor, had passed away long ago, the woman still believed she ran the town. Maybe it was the outlandish parties she threw or maybe it was the money she flaunted in excessive ways, but Mags had always made it a point to be in everybody's business.

"Cash was arrested for a DUI a few months ago," Luke revealed then shook his head. "All bogus charges that were ultimately dropped."

"DUI," Cassandra gasped. "That doesn't seem like Cash at all, not the way I remember him. I mean, he might be country music's bad boy—"

"Reformed bad boy," Luke amended. "Presley changed him."

"Yes, well. Drunk driving isn't something he would do, is it? How in the hell did he get arrested?"

"Because he was set up by Mags."

Yep. There it was. The woman who stirred up trouble. Some things never changed in this town. Surprisingly, Cassandra hadn't had a run-in with the eccentric woman since she'd been back.

"Why would she do that?" Cassandra asked.

"I'm sure she had her reasons. She's jealous

of the success of Elite Records—she wants to always come out on top no matter the cost." Luke shrugged. "Hell, who knows what she'll come up with next, but we're always on our guard with her."

Cassandra knew Mags was powerful, but for the woman to take on all of the Sutherland brothers… well, that was ridiculous. That would be a battle Mags would definitely lose.

"None of that is important now," Luke added. "I really don't want to ruin the day with talk of Mags."

"Fine by me," Cassandra agreed. "So how long are we riding?"

Luke glanced her way and winked. "We're almost there."

Confused, Cassandra glanced around and saw nothing other than the pond. She turned her attention back to Luke.

"Where?"

He gestured up ahead. "Right over there."

He took the lead with his stallion and circled the pond. That's when she saw a display that made her gasp.

"Lunch is served."

Luke dismounted his horse and looped the reins to the post next to the pond. When he came over to her, he reached up and gripped her waist to assist her down. Cassandra was so stunned by the blanket, the basket and the wine chilling in a pewter bucket, she didn't notice the way her body slid right against his until she found herself gripping his shoulders.

Luke's eyes met hers and he smiled. "I figured that even though you're a big city wedding planner now, that country girl is still inside and you'd find a picnic by the pond romantic."

Cassandra's breath caught in her throat. "Is that why we're here? Romance?"

His dark eyes locked with hers and that bond they'd formed long ago was still there. It couldn't be denied. Whatever was happening had started the second she'd stepped into his office a few weeks ago. As much as Cassandra thought she'd been in control of this entire situation, she realized right then that she hadn't grasped an ounce of control.

"I know you don't want a fling," he told her. "I didn't bring you here to seduce you or anything else, but I do know you're a romantic at heart and I thought since you were wrapped up in the wedding and—"

Cassandra kissed him.

She'd cut off whatever he was saying with her lips because she couldn't stand another second of not touching him. Luke churned something deep inside her that had been dormant for eight years. Only this man could convince her to ignore the alarm bells going off in her head and finally take what she'd been craving.

Cassandra intended to do just that.

Ten

The last thing Luke expected was for Cassandra to suddenly kiss him like she'd been just as achy as he had been. Had he known a horse ride and a picnic would have her practically climbing up his body, he would have done this weeks ago.

Luke wrapped his arms around her and splayed his hands over her back, pulling her flush against him.

Finally.

This wasn't a quick kiss or something for a social-media post. This was Cassandra taking charge, taking what they both wanted.

And if nothing else came from this kiss, then

Luke would still be okay. All he'd wanted to know was if they still had those embers between them... he hadn't expected the flames.

Cassandra framed his face and shifted, taking the kiss deeper as she sighed. Arousal and anticipation slammed into him and Luke gripped her backside and positioned their hips just right.

She pulled away from the kiss, panting and looking at him as if waiting for him to do something. But this was the one time he had to relinquish control. She'd made it apparent that a fling or anything else was off the table. He respected her enough to let her take the lead...though he would be more than willing to follow anywhere she wanted to take him.

"Are you sure you didn't bring me here to seduce me?" she asked.

"That wasn't my intention, and if we're making accusations, you've been seducing me since you came back into town."

Cassandra's eyes widened as her tongue darted out and licked her bottom lip. "I didn't come back for that...or any of this."

He waited because those murmured words that had fallen from her damp, swollen lips led him to believe she wasn't done with her thoughts.

She closed her eyes and shook her head. "But I want you. It's a ridiculous fight that I've been losing for weeks."

Some sense of calm eased into his chest. He hadn't realized he'd been waiting on her to admit that, but he had. While he'd wanted Cassandra since she'd come back, he also still cared about her. He would never push her out of her comfort zone or make her feel like she wasn't fully respected.

At the same time, he also had to be true to himself and honest with her about how he was feeling. Not that he was one to dig deep and get in touch with his emotions, but damn it, she pulled out things he thought he'd buried long ago.

"You do something to me, Luke." Cassandra opened her eyes and refocused on him. "No matter what has happened in the time I was gone, that doesn't change what we shared and what I want now."

She'd summed up his thoughts exactly. Luke reached up and slid his fingertip along her forehead, smoothing her hair back behind her ears. She shivered beneath his touch as he trailed along her jawline and down the column of her neck.

Cassandra kept her eyes locked on his and his heart pounded even faster. Was she ready to cross that line? Because he'd mentally crossed it every single day since her return. He'd give anything to know the thoughts running through her head.

"There's nothing wrong with taking what we want and there's no reason to feel guilt or worry."

Luke listened as she seemed to be talking to

herself. She reached up and traced the V of his T-shirt and he instantly held his breath.

Then he got a smile that he'd only seen back when they used to be together. It was a sexy grin that held a hint of naughtiness and a whole hell of a lot of promise.

"Tie up my horse," she commanded as her eyes remained on his. "And take a seat on the blanket."

Hell yes. She didn't have to ask him twice. Luke secured the stallion with the other horse before sinking down onto the large, soft quilt that had been left out here with their picnic.

Cassandra came to stand above him and kicked off her boots, then she went for the waist of her riding pants and slowly, so agonizingly slowly, eased them down her thighs and ultimately kicked them aside. She stood there in a plaid button-up shirt that hit just below her panties and he'd never seen a sexier sight than this woman with her hair disheveled from the ride and those long, dark legs that were just begging for his touch.

"Are you sure?"

He couldn't believe he was pausing to ask, considering she was half-naked, but he wanted zero regrets after this.

Cassandra quirked an eyebrow and started at the top button, easing each button through its hole as she continued to stare at him in silence. Of all the scenarios he'd envisioned since Cassandra had returned, this was definitely not one of them.

As if he hadn't found her sexy enough be-fore, now she was taking charge, taking what she wanted on her terms. Looks only went so far and confidence was absolutely everything. Cassandra had never faltered in that category.

She eased off the shirt and let it fall to the blan-ket. Wearing only her white lacy bra and panties, she dropped to her knees and started tugging off his boots. He jerked his shirt up and over his head and they both reached for the button on his jeans at the same time.

Their eyes met and she gave him that saucy smile once again and it had him laughing. Damn, she was something and he was not about to waste this moment.

In a flurry of hands and a few chuckles, they had his jeans and boxer briefs stripped off and tossed aside without a care. Now she remained on her knees staring down at him and Luke wanted nothing more than to reach for her and pull her on top of him. Instead, he used every ounce of will-power to keep his hands to himself.

But that didn't mean he couldn't get his point across.

Luke leaned back and laced his hands behind his head as he kept his attention on her. He smiled, waiting on her to make her next move.

Without moving her gaze, she reached around and unfastened her bra, then eased it down her arms and off to the side. Then she wiggled out of those flimsy excuse for panties.

Luke didn't even try to hide the fact he was raking his gaze over her bare body. It had been too damn long since he'd seen her like this. She was still breathtaking, still stunning, still the sexiest woman he'd ever seen.

Her curves had filled out more than he recalled. The flare of her hips and the dip in her waist were more accentuated than before, and that young woman he'd fallen in love with had turned into a strong, confident, damn fine woman. And for now, for right now, she was his.

Cassandra rested her knees on either side of his hips and straddled his lap, flattening her hands against his chest. The wind kicked up and sent her hair dancing around her shoulders. He'd never seen a more beautiful sight. His heart tightened and he refused to dwell on the feeling. His heart was just getting confused with the past, but his mind knew full well what this was…and what this wasn't.

"Tell me you don't have workers who are going to come out here anytime soon," she laughed.

"They're paid well to set up and then leave."

He couldn't wait another moment to touch her. Luke gripped her hips and eased her right where he wanted her.

"I don't have protection with me," he told her. "I honestly wasn't planning on this."

She slowly rocked against him, very nearly sinking into him, but was clearly relying on her willpower, as well.

"I don't have anything, either, but you are the only person I've ever not had it with."

He shouldn't have let his ego swell at that statement, but he did. She trusted him, in the past and now.

"I've always been careful, too," he told her.

He said nothing else as she joined their bodies, then immediately closed her eyes and tossed back her head. The way she remained still and tightened her entire body around him had Luke groaning and unable to restrain himself anymore.

Jerking his hips, he set the pace and continued to hold on to her. Cassandra shifted and leaned forward, placing her hands on either side of his head. Luke tipped up his head just enough, silently seeking her mouth. She didn't hesitate to cover his lips with hers as she started moving even faster.

This was the passionate Cassandra he'd missed. No matter the distance between them over time, this was so familiar…almost like coming home.

But that couldn't be, and it sure as hell wasn't something he wanted to be thinking about while entering this moment. He didn't want to think of the future or wish for more from Cassandra. All he wanted was this, right now. He couldn't mentally or emotionally afford anything else.

Luke flattened his hand on the small of her back and fisted her hair with the other hand. He nipped at her lips as her body jerked even harder. She released his mouth and cried out, then bit down on her bottom lip as if she'd just realized she was losing control.

"Let go," he demanded.

Her back arched and she came undone. Strands of wayward hair clung to her neck, her bottom lip, and she cried out as her knees squeezed against his sides.

Luke couldn't take his eyes off her. Damn, he'd missed her. How the hell could this be happening? He only wanted a temporary fling, one last bit of time with her before she vanished again for good.

Before he let his mind travel too far down a dangerous path, Luke's body climbed and he pumped his hips faster, harder, until he followed Cassandra over the edge.

Eleven

"No regrets?"

Cassandra reached for a piece of cheese and met Luke's gaze over the picnic lunch he'd set up while she'd gotten dressed.

"Regrets? No." She chose a cracker and took a bite before finishing her thoughts. "I was fighting the inevitable. I guess my only concern is what now? I like plans, you know, and I like to know what's going to happen. This is out of my comfort zone."

Luke chuckled. "You seemed pretty damn comfortable a few minutes ago."

Cassandra couldn't help but smile. Oh, she'd

been quite comfortable, but that was all physical. Mentally she was a hot mess. For someone who made a career out of planning every single detail down to the minute, not knowing what was going to happen between her and Luke was rather unsettling.

But there was no way she could regret the sex. Intimacy with Luke had always been the best, and the eight years between them had only made it even better.

Her heart fisted. Maybe part of her wished she hadn't let down her guard, but common sense prevailed…barely. They'd had sex. Amazing, outdoor sex, complete with a picturesque background and a romantic picnic.

Luke claimed he hadn't planned for this to happen, and she believed him, but the day couldn't have been any more romantic. Even if she hadn't been in the business of love and happily-ever-afters, she would still have found this moment to be one of the sweetest, most tender, most passionate in all her life.

So how was she just going to leave when the time came? Luke had reopened that spot in her heart she'd thought she'd sealed off. Cassandra hadn't expected her heart to open up, or those deeper emotions to rise to the surface, but they were. And now there was no way to protect herself. He would still never give her the marriage and commitment she wanted. There was no reason for her to allow herself to think otherwise.

So while her heart would be aching when she left town, at least she'd had this physical connection with him one last time. That was something, right?

"I'm not sorry we did this," she told him. "Given our past and the close bond we've always shared, I am comfortable with you. It's strange, even after all this time, that I still trust you with my body."

Luke shifted to lie on his side and propped himself up on his elbow. He'd still not put on his shirt, which was certainly not helping Cassandra's mental state. He'd left his jeans unbuttoned and now he was just lying there with all of that excellent muscle tone on display. Between the naked chest and the scruffy beard and her still tingling body, Cassandra's clothes nearly melted right back off.

"There was a time you trusted me with more than your body," he reminded her.

Cassandra stilled, then set down her food on a napkin. She wasn't sure what to say to that statement, but she needed to defend herself. Bringing up the past again wasn't something she wanted to do, but considering what had just happened, she supposed there was no other choice. Their past was what had brought them here today.

"I trusted you with everything." Cassandra swallowed the lump in her throat and shifted to cross her legs in front of her. "I would've done anything for you."

"Except stay."

"You know why I didn't."

Now he rose up and rested on his hand, his eyes holding hers in place. "Yeah, I do. I wasn't ready to marry, Cass. I had too many things going on, too much I wanted to do with my career, and I wasn't in the same place you were. I thought we were both chasing our own dreams first."

"We were," she agreed. "Until your dream became all you could see. I became invisible and what I wanted wasn't on your agenda."

That muscle ticked in his jaw as he continued to stare at her. Maybe her comment sounded selfish, but she couldn't just negate how she'd felt at that time.

"Never once did I think you were invisible," he insisted.

Hearing him say that now didn't help. She'd wanted those words then, she'd wanted him to fight for them, for what they'd planned together. But he'd been stubborn or preoccupied or something, because when she'd walked out, he'd let her go.

"You were so worried about your bars and everything going along with that, I was getting pushed farther and farther away from your priorities. And when I asked you what was more important, you said nothing. That's all the answer I needed to know. I didn't compare."

He leaned in closer as his lips thinned. "Did you ever think that I was trying to build a solid foundation for our lives? So that way when I was emotionally ready, I could give you everything you ever wanted?"

Cassandra listened and couldn't deny the passion, the frustration in his tone. Why hadn't he told her that back then? Why did he have to be so damn stubborn?

With a sigh, Cassandra reached for her stemless glass of wine and swirled the contents.

"Rehashing everything now won't change the people we were or are," she told him. "And if that's really what you were thinking back then, you should have said as much instead of letting me walk out."

"I didn't say anything because if you were hell-bent on leaving, then nothing I did or said would have stopped you," he countered. "I shouldn't have had to beg you to stay."

"No, but I deserved more than silence."

Cassandra's heart tightened again at the flash-back of that moment as she recalled the ache. She wanted out of this conversation and off this topic. Because no matter what was said now, it wouldn't erase the years of pain they'd endured, or the outcome of their relationship.

"My mom says everything happens for a reason."

The reminder that she'd left his family as well as him just layered on more pain.

Cassandra smiled despite her inner turmoil. "How are your parents? I can't believe I haven't seen them yet."

"Oh, they're dying to see you," he laughed. "And, just a heads-up, they aren't convinced that our engagement is fake."

Cassandra glanced to her ring, then back to Luke. "Why is that?"

"Probably because my parents have always loved you, but I told them this isn't going anywhere."

Before she could comment, his cell chimed. Part of her hoped he would ignore it, but he shifted to pull the phone from the pocket of his jeans.

Luke stared at the screen and sighed before setting his phone to the side. Cassandra couldn't help but look at the screen, and she saw the name *Emma*.

"Friend of yours?" she asked.

He shrugged and didn't say a word. Irritation now had Cassandra sitting up a little straighter.

"Are you still getting many calls since we started this charade?" she asked.

"Not as many, but still more than I'd like," he replied.

Luke searched through the basket of food, then pulled out a small plate of brownies and placed them on the blanket between them. Cassandra had suddenly lost her appetite.

"How about at the bar when I'm not around?"

Cassandra couldn't help but ask. She really had no right to probe and no claim to him because all of this was only a farce. But moments ago, when they'd been as close as ever, that had felt too damn real.

"The attention at the bar has definitely not slacked off," he chuckled.

That low, sultry laugh of his pissed her off even more.

Again, though, she knew she had no right. They were doing each other favors, and apparently, he rather enjoyed having the extra attention. Maybe, in spite of what he'd said when he'd asked her to become his fake fiancée, he liked living with his new title of Most Eligible Bachelor.

If that's what he wanted, then Cassandra had no place to say a word.

"Does this bother you?" he finally asked, looking back to her.

"What?"

He cocked his head, looked toward the phone and raised his eyebrows.

"Fine," she conceded. "It bothers me."

There, she'd said it. But she didn't want him to

get the wrong idea. She wasn't about to admit any more of her feelings. She was done being vulnerable for the day.

"If we're supposed to be engaged, then you should respect me enough to play the part."

"You think I don't respect you or is that jealousy talking?"

Cassandra tipped her chin. "I'm not jealous," she insisted.

"No? Then why do you care who wants to be with me or who I talk to?"

Why indeed?

"I rarely date because I spend all my time with my family or with my businesses," he went on. "I sure as hell am not advocating for the attention of these women. I run successful bars and restaurants, I make music careers, so chatting and being overly friendly are part of my job."

Cassandra listened to him and let out a sigh as she shook her head. "Maybe I am jealous, but I know I have no right or reason to be."

Luke met her gaze and she saw that hunger she'd seen countless other times. Every time he looked at her beneath those heavy lids, she wondered how they hadn't worked out the first time. How they couldn't have just lived on their attraction. She thought about how damn well they got along when they only let their bodies do all of the communicating.

He reached across and swiped his thumb along her bottom lip.

"What would you say if I told you I love the idea that you're jealous?"

Instinctively, the tip of her tongue flicked at the pad of his thumb. That fire in his eyes burned even brighter and arousal nearly consumed her.

"Luke," she murmured.

He blinked and eased his hand away, pulling them both from the moment.

"We both know this can't go anywhere." His words seemed to ground out through gritted teeth. "No matter how much I want more of you, no matter if you're jealous or not. We're still in different places in our lives."

He was right and they both knew what was at stake here.

"So what do you suggest?" she asked.

He gestured toward the brownies. "Chocolate."

Cassandra eyed the plate and couldn't help but chuckle at the switch from desire to dessert. "Are these your mother's?"

Luke let out a bark of laughter. "They're her recipe, but I made them."

"You made them?" Her focus snapped back to Luke. "When we were together before you didn't know how to do much in the kitchen."

His face sobered. "A great deal has changed since you left."

On the contrary. Cassandra feared not much had changed at all because she was starting to feel too much while Luke was still not ready for anything real.

Nothing had changed after all.

Twelve

With the wedding now only days away, Cassandra had officially hit panic mode. Every wedding she worked on had her nervous, but those nerves were always the giddy kind, filled with anticipation.

This was the first time she'd been a bundle of unidentifiable energy. Maybe that was because she was doing the wedding of someone with Hannah Banks's stature, or maybe it was because she was back in Beaumont Bay once again.

Or perhaps it was because she still couldn't get that romantic, sexy man out of her head.

Cassandra hadn't seen Luke in person for a couple of days, since he'd surprised her with the picnic. He'd texted a few times, but she kept telling him she was too busy to come up to the bar.

In truth, she was not only too busy, but she was also forcing herself to put some distance between them.

With the wedding happening in less than a week, that also meant Cassandra would be going back to Lexington soon. And once she was back home, working on building Be My Guest, she would have to put Beaumont Bay and Luke Sutherland out of her life for good.

Cassandra glanced to the piano and vowed that she would play later with a glass of wine once she could unwind and relax. For now, though, she had to get to the lake to meet with the florist and finalize plans. Then after that she had to follow up with the security detail because this wedding could not be crashed by unwanted paparazzi.

As she closed her computer, Cassandra checked her cell and calculated how much time she had before she had to get down to the gazebo by the north end of the lake. Not for another hour, which would be just enough time for—

The penthouse alarm echoed and had Cassandra jerking her attention toward the door. The only visitor she ever had was Luke. Her heart pounded and she pulled in a shaky breath. She couldn't dodge him forever, she just had to remember to keep her clothes on this time.

Cassandra crossed the spacious room and flicked the two locks before opening the door.

"Dana," she exclaimed.

"Oh, my darling."

Dana Sutherland barely got the words out before she threw her arms wide and pulled Cassandra in for an embrace. Thrilled to see Luke's mother after all this time, Cassandra returned the hug.

After a moment, Dana eased back and smiled.

"You are even more beautiful than the last time I saw you," she declared. "I hope this isn't a bad time, but I kept asking Luke to bring you to the house and he clearly has ignored me."

Cassandra stepped back and gestured. "Come on in. I have an hour to spare."

"Working on the big wedding, I assume."

Cassandra led Dana into the sitting area and took a seat on the sofa. "Are you ready for this?"

"I can't wait to finally gain a daughter," Dana replied. "Hannah is so perfect for Will. Then again, I thought you were perfect for Luke at one time."

Is that why Dana had stopped by? To prod at the current status of Cassandra and Luke's relationship?

"That wasn't meant to be," Cassandra told her. "But Hannah is so lovely. You're all very lucky to have her join your family."

"Presley is an amazing woman, too. I can't believe I'm gaining two daughters in such a short time." Dana crossed her legs and rested her arm on the edge of the sofa. "So tell me all about your life in Lexington. Luke tells me you've branched out on your own and started a wedding business."

"I did, which is why Hannah and Will's wedding is so important. This will not only be my first high-society event, this will be the first for Be My Guest."

Dana smiled. "What an adorable name. I love it. Now, tell me if I'm overstepping, but do you plan on sticking around the Bay or are you set on going back to Lexington?"

Cassandra couldn't help but laugh. "I built a life for myself in Kentucky. I have friends, and when I get back I have interviews set up so I can start adding employees because I'm hoping this wedding blows up my new business."

"I'm quite confident it will," Dana assured her. "Hannah has told me what a dream you have been to work with. She will most certainly give you a glowing recommendation to anyone who seeks your assistance."

That's what Cassandra was counting on. The possibilities were endless. This was everything she had ever wanted. A reputable wedding company of her own and a solid foundation that would lead to growth. When she'd left Beaumont Bay years ago, she'd struggled both emotionally and financially. But over time, she had gotten stronger in both areas and now she had every intention of pushing forward. Looking back on any aspect would only put a dark cloud of doubt over her dreams.

Dana gasped and pulled Cassandra from her thoughts.

"That ring…"

Cassandra glanced to her hand and back to Dana, who was still staring with the oddest look on her face.

"Are you all right?" Cassandra asked.

Dana blinked and shifted her focus. "What? Oh, um, yes. I just… That ring is beautiful."

That vise squeezed tighter around Cassandra's heart. She'd worn this ring for a couple of weeks, and as foreign as it had felt before, now she was getting more and more used to the band. Luke had really outdone himself on a ring that wasn't supposed to mean anything.

"It's quite something," Cassandra agreed. "I've seen so many different rings in my line of work, but there's something so simple and elegant about this one that really makes a statement."

Dana still seemed stunned, as if the ring in question had shifted something within her. Cassandra had no clue what was going on in her mind.

"It's really great to see you again," Cassandra stated. "Do you want something to drink or anything?"

Dana shook her head. "Oh, no, no. I just stopped

in to see you. I don't want to take up too much of your time. But I would kick myself if I didn't speak my mind while I had the chance."

Cassandra braced herself. She knew what was coming, but she loved and respected Dana enough to listen.

"I don't think you coming back to the Bay is a coincidence," she began. "I know you wanted this job, I know my son propositioned you into some ridiculous fake engagement, but I've always believed everything happens for a reason."

"I would agree with that to some extent," Cassandra replied.

Dana eased forward on the sofa and turned to face Cassandra even more. She reached over and patted her knee, while offering that motherly smile that was a precursor to advice.

"I can't help but think you two have been given a second chance," Dana said with utter conviction. Cassandra almost wanted to believe the words. "What if this is where you are supposed to be? What if Luke never got over you?"

She couldn't help but let out a soft laugh. "Luke is getting along just fine without me. All he ever wanted was those bars and to make a name for himself. He's done all of that."

"But at what cost?" Dana countered. "He's still got a void in his life, and as his mother, I can tell you that he was a disaster when you left."

"That would make two of us," Cassandra said, defending her actions. "But I couldn't stay."

Dana nodded. "I understand and nobody blamed you. In fact, we all pretty much told him to go after you and get his priorities straight."

Clearly that hadn't happened and Cassandra had actually waited for exactly that. Not to mention he'd pretty much refused to marry her.

Though she'd wanted him to fight for her, she hadn't been playing a game or leaving to get him to chase her. She hadn't issued an ultimatum because she was being a difficult girlfriend. She truly needed to remove herself from the place where she felt she was no longer appreciated. But she had honestly thought he *would* have fought for her…for them.

"Have you two discussed what happened?" Dana asked, then sighed. "I'm sorry. I don't like to be a meddling mother, but I just can't help it when I know you and Luke were so right together."

"We were," Cassandra agreed. "And then we weren't. It happens. People grow apart and move on."

Dana tipped her head and smiled, but the gesture didn't quite reach her eyes. Cassandra loved this woman like her own family and would have loved to be considered one of her daughters, but there were some things that just weren't possible.

"Would you like to join me this afternoon?"

Cassandra offered. "I'm meeting with the florist and finalizing security down by the gazebo."

"Oh, I don't want to get in the way."

Cassandra came to her feet. "Nonsense. You're the mother of the groom. Maybe after we can grab a late lunch at the new little café on the water."

Dana nodded and rose. "I would actually love that. Travis is out at an open house all day, so I could use some girl time."

Cassandra was excited to spend more time with Dana. They'd once been so close, and when Cassandra had left Luke, she'd been heartbroken over leaving all of the Sutherlands. Now if only she could remember that this, too, would be coming to an end in less than a week.

"Luke, darling."

He turned at the familiar, grating tone and found himself face-to-face with Mags Dumond. Her hot pink smile widened when he met her gaze.

"Mags," he greeted.

She glanced around the rooftop bar, seemingly scanning for something, before she focused back on him.

"Do you have a private area where I can meet with a potential new client?" she asked. "We don't want to be disturbed."

Luke resisted the urge to laugh. Maybe coming to a rooftop bar where there was nightly music wasn't the best place to have a business meeting. Then again, nobody understood Mags or her way of thinking.

He was actually surprised she'd shown up here considering it wasn't long ago she had set up Cash with a bogus DUI charge. Luke wasn't quick to forgive and forget. But he was in the business of making money and he sure as hell would take hers as a patron.

"I have a VIP room," he offered. "There's a two-hundred-dollar fee up front, but you will have a special menu and your own private bartender."

She pursed her lips and ultimately nodded. "Sounds perfect. Show me the way and then you can send my guest back. Her name is Sandra Collins."

Sandra Collins. Luke had heard of her. Her agent had actually contacted Luke about Sandra playing at The Cheshire, but he hadn't heard her music yet so he hadn't made any final decision. Luke figured Mags was here just to be her usual, busybody self and show off the fact that she was adding new artists to her label.

Since Hannah had left to sign with Will's label, Elite, Mags had been out for blood.

Luke motioned for one of his employees to come over.

"Marcus will take care of you," Luke assured Mags. "Let him know if you need anything at all."

"Wonderful." She started to turn and follow Marcus, but glanced back to Luke. "Oh, will you be open on Saturday?"

"Saturday? Of course. Why?"

"Well, with the wedding and all, I wasn't sure. I plan on having another meeting."

"My staff will take care of you, but I, of course, will not be here."

Her smile thinned. "Of course. Give my blessing to the happy couple."

As she walked away, Luke nearly groaned.

Her blessing? What the hell? Hannah and Will could care less what Mags thought or said about their nuptials…hence the reason she wasn't invited to the wedding. It was likely she just wanted to raise his awareness of that fact because her ego had taken a hit at being snubbed.

"Mr. Sutherland?"

He turned to see a fortysomething lady with a drink in hand and smile on her face…and in an extremely low-cut dress.

"Yes?"

"My name is Tracy." She held up her cell phone. "Could I get a quick picture with you? My best friend couldn't make it tonight and I promised I'd send her a selfie."

Before he could politely deny the photo, Tracy leaned in, held up the phone, and snapped a picture. Luke stepped away and offered her a smile, trying not to be rude, but also trying to respect his "fiancée's" wishes about playing the part that he had created for himself.

"My fiancée might not like you posting a picture of us on social media," he half joked.

Tracy immediately glanced down to her phone, obviously not worried about what Luke was saying. She was already sending out the photo.

Luke slipped away and headed to his back office, needing to escape for a bit before he introduced the band in an hour. They should be arriving anytime to set up, but they were return guests, so Luke had put one of his staff out to greet them.

Right now, he needed a reprieve.

Earlier he'd met his brothers for their final suit fittings and Luke had been warned that his mother had spent the day with Cassandra. Nothing good could come from that. Luke was well aware of how his mother loved Cass. Will had given Luke a heads-up, since Hannah had met the other ladies at the gazebo this afternoon.

Luke took a seat at his desk and leaned back in the chair. Rubbing a hand over his beard, he let out a sigh. Part of him didn't want Cass to leave after the wedding, but the other part knew the sooner she was gone, the sooner he could get back to his normal life. Maybe he'd start making time for dating again. Maybe he'd do more socializing outside of work.

Those ideas were all well and good, but none of them seemed to settle right within his mind.

His cell vibrated in his pocket and he pulled it out to see Cash's name with a photo attached. Luke opened the text and groaned. There was a photo of Cassandra, Hannah, and his mother all laughing and enjoying lunch. Obviously, this had come from earlier today and the caption read:

All in the Family

Of course. How lovely this image was, as it relayed assumption that everyone was one big happy family. Appearances could be convincing, but the more Luke studied that photo, the more his heart flipped in his chest.

He couldn't quite describe what he was feeling while looking at this, but he did know he had a sense of… Hell, he couldn't put a label on it. All he knew was that this was a scene that could have been his life—*his real life*—had he been ready.

At one time, his mother and Cassandra had been extremely close and they would have planned an amazing wedding. Dana had loved Cass like her own daughter, but Luke just couldn't quite commit at the speed they seemed to want him to. He couldn't be sorry about how it had ended, because he'd been true to himself. Had he given in to what everyone else wanted, he would have lost himself along the way and resented Cassandra and their relationship.

No doubt his mother had enjoyed their day out together today. He hoped she didn't get too heart-broken when Cassandra left town again.

The fact that she wouldn't look back once she was gone kept playing over and over in his head. This was it. Their last time to be together.

Luke stared at his phone another minute before he got to his feet and went out to talk to a few members of his trusted staff. He had plans and nothing was going to keep him from what he should have done long before now.

Luke had more of a solid foundation than he'd ever thought possible. He was much more advanced in his career and in a better position to have a life he could be proud of.

He wanted Cass back in his life.

Thirteen

Finally.

Cassandra dried off from her relaxing bubble bath and slid on her pink silk robe. She picked up her glass of wine from the edge of the bathtub and headed down the hall and into the living room.

The one-way windows provided a breathtaking view of the lake and all the lights of the homes and businesses while giving her the privacy she needed. Taking a seat at the piano, she set her glass on the top and lifted the cover to expose the keys.

This was what she'd been waiting to get to all day. A perfect relaxing ending to a fun, productive day.

Not only was everything going smoothly for the wedding, but Cassandra was also thrilled she'd gotten to reconnect with Dana. The woman was just as amazing as ever and Cassandra had promised that even when she went back to Lexington, she would stay in touch.

Which only meant she'd have that loose lifeline to Luke. As much as she wanted marriage and a family of her own, she was also realizing that she would have an extended family if she and Luke reconnected. His family had been hers at one time. Who said she couldn't let that kind of family fill the part of her that wanted kids and marriage, and then accept Luke as he was, in whatever kind of relationship he was ready for? Would he want to take that next step eventually? With seeing his brothers fall in love and marry, would that make him see that he could have it all?

Just as she started to play a familiar song, the bell chimed through her penthouse. Her hands stilled on the keys. She knew who was out there. At this time of the night, there wasn't a doubt in her mind.

Cassandra got to her feet and glanced down. No need in changing. She hadn't planned on visitors and Luke probably just wanted her to come up and hear the music. Tonight, though, she planned on staying in and decompressing before the mad rush that would start rolling into the weekend.

She crossed the penthouse and went to the door, where she flicked the dead bolts. As soon as she opened the door, Cassandra smiled as Luke stood before her, but her smile faltered at the look on his face.

His eyebrows had drawn in and muscles clenched in that strong jawline, but those were nothing compared to his intense, dark stare.

"Is everything okay?" she asked.

"No, it's not."

He took a step in and Cassandra moved out of his way, then shut and locked the door behind him. When she turned to face him, he was close, so close.

And she knew that look. Aside from the fact that they'd been together for years, she knew the look of a man who was hungry for passion. Her body instantly stirred with arousal. The realization that she was only wearing an extremely thin robe that could be discarded with one expert jerk of the knot only made her desire grow.

"I can't get you out of my mind," he murmured, keeping that penetrating gaze locked on her. "I can't concentrate on work and I can't escape through social media because you're all over it. My family thinks you're amazing and you're driving me out of my mind."

Cassandra opened her mouth, but the words vanished as Luke took a step forward, then another, until her back was pressed against the door. She tipped up her head and swallowed at the vulnerability looking back at her. For the first time in her life, she finally saw the unimaginable—Luke Sutherland conflicted and vulnerably exposed.

She reached up and cupped the side of his face with her hand. His nostrils flared as he leaned in to her touch.

"I need you," he whispered. "Now."

Cassandra nodded and eased up onto her tiptoes as she wrapped her arms around his neck and pressed her lips to his.

Then Luke seemed to snap as he picked her up and carried her away from the door. Her world seemed to tip as she released his mouth and buried her face in the crook of his neck. She inhaled that familiar, woodsy cologne of his. All masculine and rugged, just like the man.

He laid her down on the oversize sofa and stood over her, raking his heavy-lidded stare down her body. Cassandra couldn't stand the wait, the torture, any longer. When her hands went to the tie on her robe, Luke reached for her and shook his head.

"Let me," he commanded.

Slowly, he pulled the silk belt until the garment came untied, then he peeled away the material from her heated skin. Cassandra arched her back, seeking more of his touch, needing him to fulfill that promise she saw staring back at her.

"You're so damn perfect," he muttered.

And she felt perfect. The way he looked at her, with more passion than she'd ever seen, made Cassandra feel beautiful, cherished and, dare she think it…loved?

Luke reached behind his back and grabbed a handful of his T-shirt, then yanked it over his head and discarded it off to the side. Cassandra watched as he continued to undress until he was completely bare before her.

She reached up for him, silently inviting him to join her. As he placed his hands on either side of her head, Cassandra shifted her legs to allow him space to settle between.

The moment he aligned their bodies, she closed her eyes and relished the feel of his weight pressing her into the cushy sofa. Cassandra brought up her knees on either side of his body and tipped up her face to nip at his chin.

"You make me want too much," he murmured as he slid his lips back and forth across hers. "I can't stop this need."

Cassandra wasn't sure if he was just talking sex or if he meant something else, but now was certainly not the time to start discussing such things. She only wanted to feel. He'd come here because he'd needed her and something clicked with Cassandra…something she thought had been forgotten long ago.

When Luke joined their bodies, Cassandra wrapped her legs around his back and locked her ankles. He rested on his elbows and covered her mouth with his as he started setting the pace. Clutching his firm, broad shoulders, Cassandra opened for him and let Luke take control. He clearly needed more from this than she knew. Never before had he shown a vulnerable side. Her Luke had always been in control, always in charge, and ready for anything life threw at him.

Something had gotten into his head, and whatever it was, he needed to exorcise it out. Cassandra had told herself not to get intimate with him again while she was here, but there was no way she could turn him away. All it took was one look, one touch, especially when he showed up looking like she was the only one who could save him.

Cassandra tightened her legs and her arms, wanting him to know that she had him. As he increased the pace, she felt her body climbing. He murmured something against her lips, but she couldn't make out the words. At this point, no words were necessary. She wanted to feel, she wanted him to take all he needed.

Luke reached down and gripped the back of her thigh, pulling her leg up even higher. That's all it took for her to come undone and cry out. Moments later, Luke followed her and his entire body tightened. Cassandra continued to hold on to him as the tremors ceased.

When Luke's body relaxed and settled heavier against hers, Cassandra stroked her hands up and down his back, silently offering comfort.

When he started to shift, Cassandra flattened her palms against him.

"Stay."

"I have to be hurting you," he murmured.

Cassandra straightened her legs a little, loving the feel of his rough hair against her silky skin. This certainly wasn't the way she had planned on spending her evening, but she wasn't about to complain. Having Luke here might just have been what they'd both needed.

"You're not hurting me," she assured him.

"I know I shouldn't have come here," he told her, easing up to look down at her. "I just—"

"This is where you belong."

She hadn't meant that the way it sounded, but she wasn't sorry she'd said the words. Cassandra wanted Luke here. Part of her needed him here. Coming back to Beaumont Bay had been terrifying, personally and professionally. She'd known coming back would open up all of those old wounds and it had. But, somehow, Luke had filled those newly exposed cracks.

She didn't know what would happen after tonight. She wasn't about to ask. All she knew was

that Luke needed her and she wasn't going anywhere yet. For the next few days, she would offer
him whatever he needed…and hope she could walk
away when the time came.

Luke stared at Cassandra sleeping with the
sheet wrapped all around her. Her dark shoulders
and one shapely leg were exposed. Her black hair
was in disarray on the stark white pillowcase.

His gut tightened. This was the only woman
who could make him second-guess everything in
his life. She made him wonder why he'd let her
walk away so long ago. She made him question
how the hell he hadn't been on the same page back
then, when all she'd wanted was to be his wife.

Why hadn't he gone after her when she left?
Why hadn't he just told her to give him time?
Maybe it was pride, maybe it was that he had been
afraid that making a commitment meant he'd lose
a part of himself.

So here they were. His mother was convinced
this was the second chance he and Cassandra deserved. Luke wasn't so sure about that. He wasn't
sure this was much more than a fling, but he had
feelings…and these feelings had nothing whatso-
ever to do with the past and everything to do with
the woman who was lying so peacefully and beau-
tifully before him.

Maybe his pride was still standing in the way,

even today. Luke wasn't ready to risk asking her to stay, to see if they could maybe try again. Putting his heart on the line like that wasn't smart when he was likely just getting too caught up in all the wedding nonsense.

Between Will and Hannah's wedding and Cash and Presley's engagement, was it any wonder he was getting confused while playing pretend with his ex?

But the intimacy he'd shared with Cassandra wasn't pretend. The posts on social media, the affection in public—those were all for show. There was so much that wasn't for anyone else, though. All of this behind the scenes was strictly for them.

Luke's eyes drifted to the ring on her hand and that did nothing to calm his nerves or ease his mind.

He'd known that ring would look stunning on her hand. He'd known she would love it because Cassandra had always been more of a romantic than someone who went for bling and flash. The pearl was absolutely the perfect choice for her.

Yet she'd already told him she'd be giving it back. He wanted her to keep it. He'd wanted her to have it since the moment he bought it eight years ago. Maybe it had been naive and pathetic of him to hold on to it.

Oh, he hadn't kept the ring because he thought she'd come back. No. He'd kept that piece locked in his safe so that every time he opened it, he would have that reminder of all he'd lost and all he'd sacrificed to have what he did today.

Luke pulled in a shaky breath and turned from the room. It was early and he knew she had a full schedule ahead. The wedding was only a few days away and Cassandra would be up to her ears in flowers, seating charts, catering questions, and rehearsals.

He went to the kitchen and started up the coffee maker. After searching through the cabinets, he found two mugs. He pulled his cell from his jeans, then sent a text and ordered breakfast to be sent up ASAP.

While waiting for the coffee, he glanced around the penthouse and spotted the piano. A glass of unfinished wine sat on top and he figured he'd interrupted her last night. He wanted to hear her play again. She had a knack for music, just like Cash and Will. Luke and Gavin hadn't gotten that talent, but they did love music, so they'd entered the industry in a different manner.

Luke went to retrieve the glass and got it washed and put away just as the coffee finished brewing. He poured a mug for himself and took a sip. That first taste of hot caffeine in the morning always did wonders for his soul.

Spending the night in Cassandra's bed also did

his soul wonders. He wanted to stay here again tonight and every other night until she left.

No, he wanted her in his bed. On his turf. He wanted to see how well she fit in…

Wait. That would be a mistake.

Taking her home, seeing her in his house, would not be smart because when she ultimately left, as he knew she would, he would have those reminders in each and every room.

Maybe he could convince her to let him stay here until she left. He wouldn't mind being closer to The Cheshire. He had to pop in to his other establishments today and do some inventory and payroll, but he mainly could be found at his favorite rooftop bar.

He had no idea what the hell he truly wanted when it came to Cass. Every scenario scared him to death, but he knew he wasn't ready to let her go.

Luke grabbed his mug and went back to the piano. He slid onto the bench, took another sip, and stared down at the keys.

"He makes coffee and plays the piano."

Luke glanced over his shoulder to Cassandra, who was leaning against the doorway coming off the hall. She'd put that silky robe back on and he knew damn well she had nothing on beneath.

"I'll take credit for the coffee, but I'm terrible with any instrument."

She padded barefoot across the marble floor

and slid onto the bench next to him. He wanted to scoop her up and take her right back to bed, but they weren't at that point in this relationship.

Hell, they weren't even in a relationship. They had great sex between them and a fake engagement. They hadn't made things work the first time they were together because he hadn't been ready for more. Was he ready now? Could he give her everything he wanted and not lose part of who he was?

Luke had to just keep pressing on with this physical relationship, enjoy her while she was here, and remember that once she was gone, he would go back to the life he had created, the life he loved. He wasn't sure what else to do and he wasn't ready to take the risk to find out. Doing so, and failing, could ruin both of their lives and he sure as hell wasn't about to do that.

"Play for me," he told her.

Cassandra turned to face him, her bed head of curls falling over her shoulder as she smiled. "What do you want me to play? I usually only play for myself and to relax."

"You look pretty relaxed." He reached up and smoothed her hair away from her face, tucking the strands behind her ear. "Play anything. I had no idea until I heard you that you were so good."

Cassandra's eyes darted to her lap, then back

up. "This was my outlet when I left. I had to do something or I would have gone insane."

He understood. He'd poured himself into his work even more than when she'd been here. Had he not, he would've gone out of his mind. Besides the fact that she had left, Luke had been berated by his entire family for letting Cass go.

She said nothing else as she adjusted her position on the bench and delicately placed her fingers on the keys. Instantly, the room filled with a soft, slow song. Cassandra closed her eyes and lost herself in the music. Luke couldn't take his eyes off her.

The longer she played, the more Luke found himself getting lost right along with her. The juxtaposition of feelings continued to confuse him. He wanted her, and not just in bed, but how was that even possible? She hadn't been in town long enough for them to even discuss their past or what had happened.

Oh, they'd touched on it, but never fully resolved anything. Should he try? Should he defend his actions? Maybe let her tell her side and really listen?

But what would that solve? Going over something that happened eight years ago wouldn't change a thing and he wasn't sure he was ready to jump back in with her. Damn it, he wanted to, but he refused to get hurt again.

Keeping part of his guard up was the only way because Cassandra had never given any indication she wanted more, or that she would even consider staying here, with him, after the wedding.

When she finished playing, she glanced back to him, but all Luke could think about was that the bed was probably still warm.

"How soon do you need to be out of here?" he asked her.

A smile spread across her face and she turned to meet his eyes. "I have a little time before I need to shower, if there's something you had in mind."

Luke got to his feet and lifted her into his arms.

"I haven't had my coffee yet," she said, resting her head against his chest.

He maneuvered down the hallway toward her room. "Oh, this is much better than morning coffee."

Fourteen

Cassandra smoothed down her dark green pencil dress. She wanted to wear something appropriate for the autumn season, but still perfect for the wedding of the year. She definitely didn't want to be flashy, as she was supposed to fade into the background.

Granted, nobody would be looking at her and that's the way things should be. As a wedding planner, her only duty was to make the entire day flawless and stay behind the scenes…almost like a magical fairy had taken over and everything just appeared as it should be.

But she would be remiss if she didn't try to

sneak in a selfie or a public kiss with Luke. They were still playing the part, after all.

But she was fooling herself.

Because they'd both fallen into this "role" a little harder than they should have. Now they were coming to the end of this tête-à-tête and she'd pack up her feelings, along with her suitcases, and be done with Beaumont Bay and Luke. That was the only way to prevent heartache again.

Cassandra glanced to the aisle and the flowers on the back of each chair cover. The flowers Hannah had chosen were absolutely perfect and the weather couldn't be more beautiful. The lighting was exactly right and their pictures were going to be stunning.

As Cassandra bustled around making sure everything was in place, she was also texting Miles at The Cheshire to make sure everything was going smoothly for the reception setup.

There were so many working parts to making a wedding go off without a hitch. Everything happened at once. But this was what Cassandra lived for. And every time she reached this moment in her job, she always thought about what her own day might be like.

Maybe that's why she excelled at her job. She treated each wedding like her own to make sure the bride and her party didn't worry about a single thing.

But would she ever have her own wedding? That ring on her finger continued to mock her. It was like Luke knew exactly the type of engagement ring she would want, but couldn't see how much marriage meant to her.

She'd actually put on her pearl earrings today to match the ring. How silly was that? She would be giving it back tomorrow and packing up to head back to Lexington. The only other reason she'd have to return to Beaumont Bay would be for another celebrity wedding.

By the time Cassandra finished making her rounds and handling final touches so everything was perfect, the five-piece orchestra started playing while the guests arrived. Hannah and Will had decided to keep the guest list small at only one hundred people.

Cassandra smiled at an usher as she walked by and made her way to the lakeside community building, where the wedding party was all getting ready. It was go time and Cassandra had to make sure each person went out on cue.

The men were on the second floor and the ladies were on the first. As Cassandra approached the side entrance that the men would be using to bypass seeing any of the ladies, she was glad to see them lined up and heading in her direction.

"Ready to go," she greeted. "You all look devastatingly handsome."

And that was quite the understatement as Will led his brothers down the walkway. Cassandra's eyes naturally gravitated toward Luke. Seeing him in a tux was quite different from seeing him in jeans and T-shirts. If she'd thought he was sexy before, that was nothing in comparison to his hair perfectly parted and fixed, that scruff along the jawline, and the broad shoulders filling out that dark jacket.

Was this how he would've looked on their wedding day had they gotten to that point? Would he ever get there?

Cassandra forced away the thoughts because this wasn't the time for a self-pity party. Hannah and Will were counting on her. Any emotions or dreams or other feelings she had regarding Luke would have to be put on hold.

But the way his eyes raked over her would certainly make concentrating difficult. He might as well have been stripping her down because she felt just as exposed. Then his gaze traveled back up her body to her face and he smiled.

Oh, what that smile did to her. There was a promise there. He'd spent the past few nights in her penthouse and he'd only left her bed just this morning. Would he be back tonight? Even though they said they would be finished after the wedding, would he want one more night?

She hoped so.

"The music has started," she told them, circling back to her job. "Do everything just like last night at rehearsal."

Will looked like he was either going to pass out or run in the other direction. She'd had an amazing track record of no runaway brides or grooms and she fully intended to keep it that way.

"Look at me," she demanded, getting right in front of his face. "Your bride looks stunning and this is the best day of your life. You ready?"

He pulled in a breath and nodded. "I didn't think I'd be this nervous."

Cassandra smiled. "You're nervous because this matters. That's a good sign. And, if it helps, Hannah is a wreck. Hallie is calming her down as we speak."

Hannah had been nearly in tears questioning everything from her cake flavors to why she wore a fascinator instead of a veil. Hallie had been the only one to talk Hannah off the proverbial ledge.

Wedding jitters were a real thing and this couple sure as hell had them. But Cassandra had been serious when she said nerves were a good thing. Will and Hannah were too in love to let anything stand in their way and nothing would stop this dynamic duo from taking on the world together.

A ping in her heart had Cassandra nearly faltering, but she pasted on a smile, pushed through and gestured toward the venue.

"Let's get this beautiful moment underway."

She stepped aside as the guys walked by. As Luke passed her, he leaned down to her ear and whispered, "I can't wait to peel that dress off you tonight."

And then he kept on walking in a line with his brothers. Mercy, those men were a force when they were all banded together like this. All sexy in their own way, wearing perfectly fitted suits with wide shoulders and devilishly handsome looks.

None of the men got to her like Luke.

And it wasn't just the other Sutherland men who didn't do it for her. Nobody since she'd left Beaumont Bay had affected her or given her those thrilling vibes like the man she'd fallen in love with when she'd lived here.

The promise for tonight that he'd left her with had her shivering despite the warm autumn breeze. Cassandra made her way to the front of the community center building and walked through the atrium and toward the rooms where the ladies had been getting ready.

When she stopped in the doorway, she couldn't help but gasp at the beauty. She'd seen Hannah before, but there was something about her radiant smile today that had Cassandra jealous of such love and happiness.

"We are ready for the grandmother and the bridesmaids."

Eleanor Banks, Hannah's grandmother and mega country-music star, grabbed the hand of the flower girl and headed out the door. The entire wedding party looked like something from a magazine...which worked out well since Cash's fiancée, Presley Cole, was getting the exclusive.

Presley was the only one Will and Hannah trusted with their special day. Cassandra knew the photographers Presley had on the premises were trusted or they wouldn't be here.

So far, so good.

"If we could have the bridesmaids line up in order," Cassandra announced.

Once they were all lined up and out the door, Cassandra walked to Hannah and took her hands.

"Your groom is waiting and the sun is shining," she told the bride. "You ordered up the perfect day."

"This wouldn't have happened without you," Hannah stated.

"Oh, you still would have gotten married, but I agree. I was your best bet for a wedding planner."

Hannah laughed, just like Cassandra had hoped she would. She'd said it to take off a little of the nervous edge.

"Ready?" she asked.

Hannah nodded and glanced back to the full-length mirror one last time.

"Travis will be waiting on you at the beginning of the aisle just like you rehearsed."

Will's father was going to give Hannah away since her father was no longer living. The entire ceremony was so sweet and perfect, Cassandra couldn't recall a wedding she'd loved working on more.

She truly only thought her own would surpass everything she'd ever done for this one. Granted, that day would actually have to happen for it to surpass anything, but for now, she was thrilled with the direction of her business.

"Thank you," Hannah told her. "I truly would have gone mad without you during all of this."

"You would have been just fine," Cassandra assured her. "Now go get married."

Hannah lifted her dress and slipped through the doorway. Cassandra double-checked again with Miles about the reception and he confirmed that all was set and ready to go. The bridesmaids should be going down the aisle now, and soon Hannah would be, too.

All was right and Cassandra made her way toward the gazebo area. She remained in the background as the ceremony took place. She couldn't help but watch Luke at the end of the aisle as he stood next to his brother. At one time in her life, she had pictured him waiting on her as she glided to his side in a designer dress. She envisioned him tearing up or smiling and telling her how beautiful she looked.

None of that was real, though. As Cassandra glanced at the ring on her finger, she couldn't help but wish second chances weren't just for fairy tales.

Fifteen

"What is she doing here?" Cash asked. "This reception is family and close friends only."

Luke turned toward the elevator and spotted Mags as she stepped off. She waved to someone and instantly lifted a champagne flute off the tray of a passing waiter.

"Hell if I know, but I'll take care of it."

He maneuvered through the small crowd and approached the unwanted guest. She caught his eye and had the nerve to smile like everything was perfectly normal with her crashing a wedding reception.

"What a beautiful wedding," Mags declared as he came closer.

"You weren't invited. How would you know?"

Mags laughed and took a sip of her champagne. "Luke, darling, Hannah is a stunning bride. I can see her from here. And that woman of yours outdid herself. Who knows, maybe if I marry again, Cassandra can plan my wedding. I hear she might be busy planning yours, though."

Luke wasn't taking the bait.

"You have no reason to be here, Mags."

She jerked back, her eyebrows drawn in as if she was literally hurt.

"And I thought you had a meeting with someone today," he reminded her.

"Oh, I rescheduled. Wishing my former star all the best in this new chapter of her life was much more important."

There weren't many people who grated on his nerves, but Mags Dumond was sure as hell one of them. Will and Hannah purposely hadn't invited her and she damn well knew it. But he wasn't going to cause a scene on his brother's wedding day. He would, however, keep his eye on the busybody.

"Don't ruin their day," he warned. "You're not the only one with power."

Her eyes widened slightly and she held her free

hand to her chest. "I would never," she gasped. "I just want to give the happy couple my best wishes."

Luke snorted and moved away. The woman didn't have an innocent bone in her body. She lived to stir up trouble. She was like a walking soap opera and Luke would never forgive her for setting up Cash to get arrested for that DUI.

She'd been jealous that Hannah had left her studio to team up with Cash at Will's label. The DUI falsehood had been a petty move that no one could actually prove was Mags because she was too slick, but the Sutherland brothers knew exactly who had tried to destroy Cash's reputation.

"You're frowning."

Luke blinked and realized Cass had come to stand in front of him. He'd been preoccupied with his own thoughts, but now he shoved Mags to the back of his mind.

"Something wrong?" she asked.

Luke shook his head. "What could be wrong on this day? My brother married the love of his life in a beautiful ceremony that people will be talking about for years."

A wide smile spread across her face. "That's what I'm counting on," she told him. "I only had one minor hiccup, but I don't think anyone noticed but me."

He hadn't noticed that anything had gone wrong. All he'd seen was Cass in that body-hugging green dress that was supposed to look polished and professional, but made him think about how damn amazing her curves looked. And he couldn't wait to fulfill the promise he'd made to peel her out of it.

"You've got that look in your eyes," she murmured.

Luke eased closer and snaked an arm around her waist. "What look is that? The one that says I want to kiss you or the one that says I want to tear this dress off you?"

Cassandra's eyes darted to his mouth. "Both."

"Soon," he assured her.

"We probably shouldn't be so affectionate here," she whispered. "This is your brother's reception and I'm the wedding planner."

"And we're still engaged," he reminded her.

"This is our last day for that."

Her statement might be true, and one he'd agreed to, but that didn't mean he liked the situation. That didn't mean he was ready to give her up, take that ring back, and have it again as only a reminder of all he'd lost.

But was he ready to be vulnerable again? Was he ready to ask her to stay? Was that even fair of him? To ask her to uproot the life she'd made and move back here?

"This is a nice-looking couple."

Luke turned to see his parents both beaming

at him and Cass. Of course, they would love to see Luke and Cassandra back together, but Luke had made things perfectly clear...or at least he thought he had.

"The wedding was absolutely gorgeous," Dana said, beaming. "You really have a special talent."

Cassandra smiled and took a step away from Luke. "I love what I do, so I always hope that comes through."

"I imagine you are going to be one very busy lady after today," his mom added.

"I hope so."

Travis slapped Luke on the back and gave him a half hug. "Has my son convinced you to stay in Beaumont Bay yet?"

Luke glanced to his dad and willed the man to be quiet.

Cassandra's eyes darted from Luke to Travis and back again. "Are you going to ask me to stay?"

Luke shook his head. "Ignore them. They're still living in the past."

A flash of something moved over Cassandra's face, but he couldn't identify it and it was gone before he could truly put a label on it.

"Second chances don't always come around," his dad said. "Maybe you two should think before just parting ways."

Think? That's all Luke had been doing since Cassandra had stepped into his office. He thought of the past, he thought of the present and now he was forced to think of the future. Did he want to allow himself to be vulnerable enough to admit he wanted to try again? Would she even want to? Would she trust him with her heart again? She'd never said as much and she'd insisted she wouldn't keep the ring. Hell, she probably already had her bags packed.

"We both have such different lives now," Cassandra said. "Sometimes two people can get along perfectly, but are just not meant to be."

Luke watched as his parents exchanged a glance and he knew Cassandra was wasting her breath. Clearly, she meant what she was saying. She did not think they were meant to be anything more than what they were.

At least Luke had his answer. He would keep his feelings to himself. Disappointment and loss settled deep. He was the one who hadn't been able to commit before, so all of this pain and heartache and frustration rested on his shoulders.

But they weren't twenty-five anymore. They had set down roots and were growing each day in their journeys that took them away from each other.

"Well, a mother can hope," Dana added.

"It looks like your brother has his sights set on someone, as well," Travis added with a nod toward the corner of the rooftop.

Luke glanced up and spotted Gavin and Hallie deep in what appeared to be a serious conversation. Then Hallie shook her head and Gavin laughed. Good grief, was his brother seriously hitting on Hannah's twin? The woman looked like she'd rather be anywhere else than where she was.

"I just want to see all my boys happy," Dana said with a sigh. "And then I can start having grandbabies."

Travis chuckled. "Let's give the boys some time to adjust to being in love before you throw babies into the mix."

"The only ones in love are Will and Cash," Luke demanded. "Everyone needs to calm down."

Cassandra laughed. "Relax," she told him with a pat on his arm. "Your mother is happy and who can blame her. Today was a wonderful day."

"Just as long as she doesn't expect a wonderful day coming from me anytime soon," Luke murmured.

Damn it, he wanted out of this situation, but he couldn't exactly be rude. Thankfully, the DJ announced it was time for the first dance for the bride and groom. Everyone's attention turned to the center of the rooftop, where Will and Hannah stepped up and embraced each other with the happiest smiles Luke had ever seen.

That pang of jealousy he hadn't expected took him completely off guard. What were all of these emotions attacking him? He didn't want to be jealous or confused. He didn't want to second-guess every decision, past or present, where Cassandra was concerned.

When he glanced to her, all of her focus was on the happy couple. Cass had the softest smile on her face with tears brimming in her eyes. There was that hopeless romantic he'd fallen in love with so long ago and she paid him absolutely no mind. She had moved on and, as soon as he got that ring back, he should, too.

Cassandra had never felt more conflicted in her entire life. This wedding couldn't have gone any better. She had already received an email yesterday from a record producer in Nashville who wanted his daughter to meet with Cassandra and discuss her upcoming wedding in the spring.

Once Presley went public with this exclusive story and the first photos were sent to the rest of the media, Cassandra hoped her inbox would be flooded with so many potential weddings that she had to hire even more staff than she first intended.

Wouldn't that be something? To have to hire several staff to keep moving forward with Be My Guest.

On the other hand, as much as Cassandra was riding high now that the day was drawing to a close, she knew her time in Beaumont Bay was done. It had taken all her willpower to keep her true feelings to herself when Dana and Travis came over and were blatantly and boldly telling her to stay.

Luke hadn't mentioned her staying and he'd never acted like he wanted marriage any more now than he did before. He certainly hadn't even pretended to be jealous of his brothers and their nuptials.

As Cassandra helped work on cleaning up after the reception, she ran over every detail of the day and knew the events couldn't have gone any better. She was damn proud of herself, though she was so ready to get back to her penthouse and relax.

"Cassandra."

She turned to see Presley and smiled. "Hey. I thought you and Cash left by now."

"We wanted to help clean up," she stated. "And I stuck around for a more selfish reason."

Cassandra motioned toward one of the sofas and led Presley around Luke's employees, who were working hard on transforming the reception back into a bar.

Once they were seated, Cassandra let out a sigh and leaned back against the cushions.

"I bet you haven't sat all day." Presley laughed. "You outdid yourself with this wedding. It was beyond anything I had imagined."

"Thank you. And, yes, this is the first time I've sat, but that's my job and I love it."

Presley's bright smile widened. "That's what I want to talk to you about. I was hoping I could get on your schedule before you get too busy."

Cassandra couldn't help but return the smile. "I would never get too busy for you and Cash. Working on your wedding would be amazing. What date are you all thinking?"

"Honestly, I'm just so thrilled to be getting married, we're open. I don't want cold weather and I'd love something outdoors if possible."

Cassandra's mind started racing with the possibilities. No matter how tired she was now, she was always in the mood to get creative and plan a couple's perfect day.

"I'm sure we can come up with something amazing for the two of you," she promised. "Why don't you email me any ideas you have so far, whether it be colors or venue or even a dress style you like, just so I can get an idea of what you're thinking. Also, feel free to tell me things you absolutely do not want."

Presley clapped her hands together. "I will. Oh, my gosh, I can't believe this is really going to happen."

"Believe it. Cash is completely in love with you and he had one of the most romantic proposals I've ever seen."

Pulling Presley up on stage during one of his concerts and producing a ring from his guitar had blown up the internet and there wasn't a woman in the world who hadn't watched that clip over and over.

"You might just be the next one to make a Sutherland brother give up his bachelor status," Presley joked.

Cassandra shook her head. "I doubt it. We were just pretending, you know."

"Oh, Cash filled me in on the arrangement you and Luke made," Presley claimed. "But I've seen the way Luke looks at you and the way you look at him. I'm assuming you're both stubborn."

Cassandra laughed.

"Sorry," Presley quickly added. "I just can't help but say what I feel and it would be such a shame for the two of you to walk away from each other again when it's so obvious to everyone around you that you're meant to be together."

Why did everyone keep saying that? Of course, she and Luke were looking at each other in a certain way…likely because they were both still sexually attracted to each other and there was no hiding that. But there was no way to build a future, a lifetime, on sex or lustful glances. It didn't work the first time and it simply wouldn't work now…no matter how much she longed for Luke and that life they'd talked about. Dreams didn't always come true and there always came a moment when one had to put aside a fantasy and focus on a new dream.

"I think this whole family is so swept up in wedded bliss that they just want everyone to walk down the aisle," Cassandra joked, hoping to deflect the attention off things that could never be.

"Maybe so, but I still stand by my statement that you and Luke are too adorable together."

"Well, thanks, but we're just friends."

Friends? They hadn't actually decided to stay in that zone once she was gone. Right now, they were lovers, but after tonight… Well, she really didn't know what they would be. Likely a distant memory and the thought of never seeing him again hit her hard.

The pang of intense loss had her throat burning and her eyes stinging. Cassandra got to her feet and forced a smile.

"If you will excuse me, I have a few things to finish up here, but get me that email and we will get this wedding ball rolling."

Presley rose and looked like she wanted to say more as her eyebrows drew in. Cassandra was terrible at hiding her feelings, but she really didn't want to go further into the topic of Luke.

Ultimately, Presley nodded and Cassandra excused herself. After checking with the staff of the bar to make sure everything was under control, she made her way to the private elevator.

Once she was in her penthouse she could fall apart. Now that everything was over and there was no more reason for her to stay, every emotion came crashing down around her.

Cassandra stepped into her suite and stilled. Across the way, standing with his back to her as he glanced out at the starry night, was Luke. When he tossed a glance over his shoulder, Cassandra knew this was it. He was going to make good on that promise to peel her out of her dress and they were going to share their last night together before she left Beaumont Bay.

Sixteen

Too many emotions stirred within Luke, but he couldn't concentrate on them. They all felt too damn vulnerable, as if he was losing control. He never lost control and he sure as hell couldn't afford to now.

Raw physical need was all he could manage because at least he could remain strong and dominate that familiar territory.

The day had been long and he imagined Cassandra was exhausted. As he turned fully to face her, the weariness in her expression was apparent, but there was something else—something he couldn't quite pinpoint.

"I wasn't sure you'd wait for me," she told him as she slipped out of her heels and padded bare-foot toward him. "You must be tired."

"I was just thinking the same about you." Luke met her halfway and reached for her. His hands rested on her shoulders and he gave a gentle squeeze. "Why don't you let me take care of you now? You've done so much for everyone else."

She let out a groan as he continued to massage her. Her lids slowly lowered as her head tipped to the side. Luke touched his lips to her forehead before releasing her shoulders. Then he scooped her into his arms and headed toward the bedroom.

"I can walk," she laughed. "I'm not that tired."

"You can do many things, but right now I'm taking over."

She rested her head against his shoulder and sighed. "I like the sound of that."

So did he…more than he thought. As Luke set her on her feet and moved to her back to unzip her dress, he realized he wanted to take care of her for more than just tonight. He wanted to be the one she leaned on after her stressful days. He wanted to be the one that she turned to for every aspect of her life.

He'd been juggling her needs, this fake relationship, and his businesses just fine since she'd come into town. She knew exactly what he did and how much he put into his work, just as he knew how much she loved her own career. Why couldn't they both have it all and enjoy each other? They could support each other and work through this life together, right?

Right now, he just wanted to feel her. He wanted to show her, without words, that he had come to care for her again.

Did that mean he loved her? He'd loved her when she'd been here before, but his feelings were quite different now and he had no clue what to do with them or how to label them. One thing was certain—these feelings were much more intense, much more overpowering.

As promised, he peeled the fabric down her curvy body and left her in her black lacy bra and panties.

"And I thought you looked sexy with the dress on," he murmured, taking in the beautiful sight of her.

Cass smiled and stared up at him. "I wore this set for you," she confessed. "I was hoping you'd spend one last night with me."

One last night. That's what she had in her head…that's what he should have in *his* head. But, damn it, he didn't know if he could let her go.

That was a conversation for another time. Right now, he didn't care about words, he only cared about making her feel and clearing her mind of anything else but him.

Luke encircled her waist with his hands and lifted her. She let out a little gasp as he carefully settled her back onto the bed. She was lying there looking up at him with all of that dark hair around her. Those heavy lids had nothing to do with her being tired and everything to do with her arousal and passion.

No woman had ever looked at him the way Cassandra did. No woman had the power to make him want to relinquish every bit of control the way she did, either.

And that was new, different from when they were younger.

That was also how he knew he was in a whole hell of a lot of trouble if she ended up leaving again.

"How long are you going to stare?" she murmured.

Luke pulled from his unwanted thoughts. They had no room here, not when he wanted to solely concentrate on Cassandra.

He wasted no more time as he stripped out of the rest of his tuxedo. When she reached for him, he shook his head.

"Not yet," he told her. "Just lie back and relax."

Her hands fell to her sides as her eyes remained locked on him. Damn, he never tired of that look she gave him. This was the moment he wanted to keep locked in his mind forever…and maybe in his heart.

Luke eased back just enough to take her delicate foot between his hands. The second his thumb raked up her arch, she let out another moan. Clearly, she liked this and he'd barely gotten started.

Luke couldn't take his eyes off her as he continued to massage first one foot and then the other. He worked his way up her calves, her thighs, and that's when she began to get impatient. Her hips jerked and she whimpered.

"You're not relaxing," he chuckled, reaching for the lace scraps across her hipbones. "You seem to be a little too on edge."

"On edge?" she asked. "I'm aching, Luke. Please."

A begging Cassandra was something he'd never been able to turn down and now was no different. Selfishly, he didn't want to wait, either. He'd had to watch her all day long rushing from one area to the next, all while wearing that body-hugging dress and a sweet smile on her face.

He didn't realize how much he'd wanted her in his life until she'd come back into it.

Luke clenched his jaw to keep from saying something in the moment he might not want her to know afterward. His vulnerability was teetering on the line and he was about ready to expose himself.

Sliding her panties down her legs, Luke focused on her dark eyes. Cassandra rose up onto her elbows as he moved up her body. He reached around her back and flicked the clasp on her bra as she wiggled it off and tossed it behind her.

Luke gathered her and flipped until she was straddling his lap. Her hair went wild around her shoulders as she smiled down at him. Damn it. His heart flipped in his chest and that's exactly what he didn't want to happen.

Too late.

Flattening his hands on her thighs, Luke slid up to that crease at her hips. He gripped and jerked his hips beneath her. She instantly took his silent gesture and joined their bodies.

When she braced herself against his chest and started moving, Luke absolutely got lost in the sight. The passion from this woman, the bond they shared, wasn't something he'd felt since she'd been gone. Luke couldn't help but wonder if she was it for him. Was he just getting caught up in nostalgia and his brothers' happiness, or was Cassandra the one for him?

Luke shifted and rose, taking her legs and wrapping them around his back. She continued to move with him as he wrapped himself around her. He couldn't get close enough. He wanted her, in bed and out. He wanted some magical moment where she knew how he felt and he didn't have to bare himself completely by telling her.

Just as she started to come undone, Luke leaned in and captured her lips. He wanted to experience every single aspect of her passion as he was closing in on his own climax.

Cass trembled against him and Luke couldn't hold back any longer. He joined her as he held on, never wanting this moment to end…never wanting to say goodbye.

He was lying sleeping in her bed and she didn't have the heart to wake him. Cassandra leaned against the doorframe of the en suite and took in the man who had made love to her all night with such passion and care.

And today she would be leaving. They hadn't talked, even though that's exactly what she'd vowed to herself to do. She didn't want any heartache or ill feelings before she left. They'd found some common ground and she'd come to care for him once again. Or maybe she'd never stopped.

Regardless of her feelings, they'd created such successful lives in completely different cities. Being in Beaumont Bay for just over a month wasn't near enough for her to drop everything and stay. She'd had eight years of rebuilding and couldn't give all that up…not that he'd asked her to.

A fierce, invisible grip on her heart had her nearly tearing up. She had to remain in control of her emotions, though. She'd known this day was coming and she'd known Luke wouldn't need her anymore after the wedding.

That had been the entire plan, right? They'd both gotten what they'd wanted, had an intense fling on the side, and now they were both ready to go about their lives just like before.

Only she wasn't sure she'd ever be like before because all she'd done here was reopen all her old wounds and reach into that pocket where she'd kept her emotions regarding Luke. They'd all come spilling out and now she had to figure out how the hell to pack them all back in.

But she didn't want to pack them back in.

She wanted to leave them out, and she wanted Luke to admit he wanted her, to admit that maybe they could try for something they hadn't been ready for before. Was any of that even possible? Was all of this worth the risk?

Cassandra padded quietly into the kitchen and ordered room service. What was the protocol for saying goodbye to an old lover and fake fiancé? Surely a nice breakfast was a good start. But what was there to talk about?

The nerves seemed to pile higher and higher. Cassandra closed her eyes and took a deep breath. She needed coffee and she needed to just calm down. Luke wasn't expecting anything from her… and that was the crux of her issue right now.

Last night, she could have sworn he was going to say he loved her. Just the way he held her, the way he touched her, the man was in love. Maybe he didn't know it. Maybe he didn't want to be. Or maybe he refused to face reality.

So if he wasn't going to say anything, despite their passionate night, then she wasn't going to say anything, either.

Damn it.

Presley was right. They were two stubborn people and maybe that had been the problem all those years ago. Maybe if she'd told him what she needed from him, things would have been different. But, in her defense, she hadn't wanted to beg for attention or fall second to his work.

Several minutes later the elevator chimed, indicating a visitor, and Cassandra tightened the belt on her robe and went to the door to meet the waiter. Once she'd tipped him, she wheeled the cart inside and laughed. Maybe she'd been a little out of it when she'd called. Luke had her so confused, it looked like she'd ordered for the entire wedding party from yesterday.

"Damn, woman. How long are we staying in and eating?"

She glanced up to see Luke rubbing a hand over

his bare chest as he shuffled from the bedroom. His eyes were on the silver domed trays.

"I wasn't sure what you'd want and I really didn't know what I was in the mood for."

His eyes moved to her and there it was…that hunger. She couldn't get sidetracked, though. They'd had their last night and there were still some loose ends to tie up before she left.

"Do you want to eat first or talk?"

Luke stilled and his eyes locked onto hers. "What is there to talk about?"

Everything, but nothing she wanted to get into. She twisted the ring on her finger and ultimately slid it off.

"For starters, this is yours."

Cassandra extended her arm, but Luke just continued to stare at her. She wanted him to take it, to make their break as simple and painless as possible. After all, this had all started as a business arrangement, so shouldn't they end things that way, as well?

"I want you to keep it."

Cassandra dropped her arm and sighed. "I can't do that, Luke."

"Why not?"

Because it would remind her of what she didn't have. Because she would look at it every day and think of him, which was something she could not afford to do.

"We aren't engaged," she told him.

"Maybe not, but that ring is yours."

He took a step forward, and then another, until he stood toe-to-toe with her. Those dark eyes seemed to penetrate her, as if he could read her thoughts. That was the last thing she needed. Because no matter the gap of time that had separated them, Luke still knew her better than anyone. She'd never let anyone get as close as he had. That bond they'd shared still hadn't been severed. Despite everything, there was a piece of her heart that would always belong to Luke Sutherland.

"I suppose you're leaving today," he said, still studying her face.

Cassandra nodded, fisting her hand around the ring.

"Will you come back?" he asked.

"Come back?"

"To visit," he added. "I know my family loved seeing you and my parents said you told them you'd stay in touch."

She swallowed the emotional lump forming in her throat.

"Are you asking on their behalf or yours?"

The muscle in his jaw clenched and he took a step back, raking a hand over his jaw. The morning stubble bristled against his palm, breaking the silence surrounding them. Her heart beat so fast…

She wanted him to answer. She wanted him to tell her what he was thinking and what he wanted.

"Maybe I'm asking for both of us," he finally replied.

Cassandra truly didn't think their morning talk would get so emotional. She'd hoped he'd take the ring, they'd share breakfast, maybe a few kisses, and he'd be gone.

That wasn't going to be the case, so she had to shore up all her courage, all her willpower, to get through this. She couldn't leave town with heartache again. She didn't know if she'd survive it.

"Are you asking me to come back?"

"What if I am?" He rested his hands on his narrow hips and waited a beat. "Would you come back if I asked just for myself?"

Confused, Cassandra needed something to focus on besides these unwanted feelings. She moved to the cart and poured a mimosa. Once she had the tall, slender glass in hand, she turned back around and wrapped her arm around her waist.

"I don't want to play games," she told him. "If there's something you want from me, you need to say it. Otherwise, I should start packing."

His eyebrows rose and he let out a low, humorless laugh. "I don't want you to pack."

"Then what do you want?" she asked as her heart kicked up.

"I don't know, Cass, but I'm not ready for you to just pack and go."

Cassandra nodded and took a sip.

"The last time you broke things off and just left. There wasn't much discussion."

Unable to stand still under his penetrating gaze, Cassandra moved around the penthouse and made her way to the wall of windows overlooking the lake. She didn't like the unsettling nerves that came with her relationship to Luke. They'd been there since she walked into his office a month ago and had only grown with each passing day.

"I had to leave, Luke. I realized we were obviously wanting two different things at that time and staying would have only shattered both of us even more."

Maybe she was a coward for not facing him, but she just couldn't. They were entering into a conversation that was long overdue and even after eight years, she still wasn't ready for it.

"I had to put myself first," she added, forcing herself to turn and take this head-on. "I'm not placing the blame on you. I know it takes two people to make a relationship work. Maybe I should have told you long before that I wasn't going to be second to anything, including your work."

Luke jerked. "Is that what you thought? That you were second to my businesses?"

"That's not what I thought, that's what I know."

Luke crossed the room with purpose and stood right before her. He took her drink and set it over on the table by the sofa. Then he came back, took her fisted hand and opened her fingers.

"See that ring?" he demanded. "I chose that for you eight years ago. I intended to propose to you, so we could officially start our lives together. But I wasn't ready, not when you were. I needed time and I wasn't sure when I'd be ready for what you wanted."

"Then why didn't you fight for me?" she demanded. "Why didn't you tell me you were needing more time?"

"Because you said you were leaving and I knew if you felt that way, then there was nothing I could say. If you wanted to go, then maybe we weren't right for each other and you *should* go."

She stared at him another minute and truly didn't know what to say or what had gotten them to this heart-wrenching point.

"Damn it," he muttered as he spun around and gave her his back.

"Luke."

"Forget it."

But she couldn't forget it because now they were entering a whole new territory, one she hadn't even known they needed to explore…and she had a feeling more emotions than she ever wanted to admit were about to be exposed.

Seventeen

He'd never wanted to tell her that. He'd never wanted to admit he'd been a damn fool and had gotten her a ring and then, like the pathetic heartbroken man he'd been, he'd kept the damn thing for all of this time.

"Talk to me."

Cassandra's soft, questioning tone had Luke turning back around. He hadn't been strong enough the first time she was in his life, but he damn well would be now. Maybe this was risky, maybe this was all a mistake and he was going to end up looking like a fool again, but he had to know. He had to.

"I never put you second in my life." He held her gaze, wanting her to see he was absolutely telling the truth. "You know I invested everything I owned and took out loans to get those bars up and running. I wanted a solid foundation and a firm income before proposing to you. I didn't want to come to you before I knew I could provide the life you deserved. But then I was afraid. I feared if I took that step that I would lose myself and all I had created. I didn't know how to have it all and the risk scared the hell out of me."

Her eyes widened and instantly started brimming with tears. Luke clenched his jaw and waited for her to say something…and he also cursed the man he used to be for not standing up for what he wanted and for being too damn stubborn.

"Everything I did was because I was putting you first," he added. "But then… I just wasn't ready."

"I didn't know," she whispered.

"I was so busy trying to pave the way to an easy life for us, and then all I could think of was how I could juggle it all…and I let you go."

Cassandra blinked and a lone tear slid down her dark skin. Luke reached out, cupped her cheek, and swiped away the moisture. She leaned in to his touch.

"I never knew you were that afraid. I should've asked. I should have made you talk to me." She closed her eyes as another tear escaped. "What have we done?"

"We were guarding our hearts. That's why we didn't communicate properly."

Her lids fluttered open as she focused on him. Luke hated seeing her cry, hated knowing he'd had any part of her unhappiness and heartache.

"So what happens now?" she asked.

This was the tricky part, the hardest part…but maybe the most rewarding.

"You can decide to go as you had planned or you can decide to stay a bit longer and see how this plays out."

When she remained silent, he reached up with his other hand and framed her face.

"I would never make you decide between your life in Lexington and Beaumont Bay," he told her. "That's not fair for either of us. But if you want to make this work, we will find a way. I can go to Lexington if that's what you want. I can still own my bars, I have managers I trust to run them, and I can come down every few weeks to check on things."

"Luke."

The emotional whisper had his heart clenching. He'd gone this far, he might as well finish the rest.

"Did you look at the planner I bought you?" he asked.

Her eyebrows drew in as she shook her head.

"I mean, I looked at it, but I haven't gone through it or anything. Why?"

"Go get it."

She eased back, still looking at him like he was crazy. Hell, maybe he was crazy for putting himself on the line like this. But he hadn't gotten this far, been this successful in his life, without taking risks and putting himself out there.

Cassandra went to her bedroom and then came back out with the planner. She started to hand it to him, but he pointed to it.

"Open it to today's date," he told her.

She flipped through the pages until she came to the date. When her eyes landed on the square and the red writing he'd added, she gasped.

"'Tell Cass how much she is loved,'" she whispered.

Then her eyes darted up to his. The shock on her face made him realize he'd never seen her this shocked and that meant he'd done a terrible job of letting her know just how much he'd fallen for her all over again. He'd hoped she'd pick up on that on her own, but clearly she hadn't.

"You love me?" she asked.

Luke nodded. "I do."

"But you gave this to me weeks ago. You already knew then?"

"I'm not sure I ever stopped loving you, Cass," he told her. "When you came back, all of those old feelings came back, too, but then I started with new feelings as I got to know the new Cassandra."

"You think you know me well enough now to say those words?" she asked.

Damn it, he wanted her to say them back. But he wanted her to mean them. His heart had been exposed and he wished like hell she'd take it again.

"I know when you set your mind to something, you make it happen," he began. "I know you're a successful wedding coordinator, which was a dream you made come true. You're strong, resilient, loyal, loving to my family like they are your own, sexy as hell, and I don't want to be without you anymore."

Her eyes filled once again as she glanced back to the planner.

"Luke, I…"

She closed the planner, but kept her head down. Luke's breath caught in his throat and he had no idea what she was thinking, but he wished she'd clue him in. He'd never been so nervous or on edge in his entire life.

Finally, she glanced up to him as tears streamed down her cheeks…but she was smiling.

"I love you," she told him. "I never thought I'd get the opportunity to tell you that again, but your mom was so right. Second chances happen for a reason and this encounter happened to force us back together…where we belong."

A wave of relief washed over Luke. He hadn't been sure she felt the same—he'd hoped, he'd suspected, but he hadn't been certain.

Now he knew. And there was no way in hell he would ever let her go again.

Luke took the planner from her and tossed it over to the sofa, then banded his arms around her and lifted her. She squealed as he spun her in a circle and kissed her firmly on the mouth.

"How soon can you plan our wedding?" he asked.

She laughed. "Well, I hadn't thought of that considering we just decided to go from fake to actually engaged."

Luke sat her down, took the ring and slid it back onto her finger. "This is where my ring belongs. I'm ready now and I know with your support and love, I can have it all. We both can. Our careers and a successful relationship are what we both deserve."

"Where will we live?" she asked.

"I don't care about that, either." He honestly didn't. So long as he had her by his side. "We can discuss details later. Right now, I'm taking you back to bed."

"Shouldn't we call your family and tell them the good news?" she asked.

Luke scooped her up into his arms and headed

back toward the bedroom. "I have more important things to do, like make love to my fiancée."

Her smile widened as she looped her arms around his neck. "Presley was right. She said I'd make you fall for me. Now there's only one Sutherland left."

Luke laughed. "No way in hell will Gavin settle down. My mom better be happy with the three new daughters she has."

Cass started to open her mouth again, but Luke tossed her onto the bed, then climbed in after her.

"No more talk." He came to settle over her, his heart completely full of more than he'd ever thought possible. "Let me show you just how much I love you."

She smiled. "Kiss me again."

* * * * *

*Don't miss the final book in the
Dynasties: Beaumont Bay series*

Good Twin Gone Country
by Jessica Lemmon

Available next month!

COMING NEXT MONTH FROM

⊕HARLEQUIN
DESIRE

#2815 TRAPPED WITH THE TEXAN
Texas Cattleman's Club: Heir Apparent • by Joanne Rock
To start her own horse rescue, Valencia Donovan needs the help of wealthy rancher Lorenzo Cortez-Williams. It's all business between them despite how handsome he is. But when they're forced to take shelter together during a tornado, there's no escaping the heat between them...

#2816 GOOD TWIN GONE COUNTRY
Dynasties: Beaumont Bay • by Jessica Lemmon
Straitlaced Hallie Banks is nothing like her superstar twin sister, Hannah. But she wants to break out of her shell. Country bad boy Gavin Sutherland is the one who can teach her how. But will one hot night turn into more than fun and games?

#2817 HOMECOMING HEARTBREAKER
Moonlight Ridge • by Joss Wood
Mack Holloway hasn't been home in years. Now he's back at his family's luxury resort to help out—and face the woman he left behind. Molly Haskell hasn't forgiven him, but they'll soon discover the line between hate and passion is very thin...

#2818 WHO'S THE BOSS NOW?
Titans of Tech • by Susannah Erwin
When tech tycoon Evan Fletcher finds Marguerite Delacroix breaking into his newly purchased winery, he doesn't turn her in—he offers her a job. As hard as they try to keep things professional, their chemistry is undeniable...until secrets about the winery change everything!

#2819 ONE MORE SECOND CHANCE
Blackwells of New York • by Nicki Night
A tropical destination wedding finds exes Carter Blackwell and maid of honor Phoenix Jones paired during the festivities. The charged tension between them soon turns romantic, but will the problems of their past get in the way of a second chance at forever?

#2820 PROMISES FROM A PLAYBOY
Switched! • by Andrea Laurence
After a plane crash on a secluded island leaves Finn Steele with amnesia, local resident Willow Bates gives him shelter. Sparks fly as they're secluded together, but will their connection be enough to weather the revelations of his wealthy playboy past?

YOU CAN FIND MORE INFORMATION ON UPCOMING HARLEQUIN TITLES, FREE EXCERPTS AND MORE AT HARLEQUIN.COM.

HDCNM0721

"Listen." Carter broke the silence when they reached her door. "I didn't mean to upset you."

Phoenix cut him off. "Don't worry about it."

"I thought the timing was right. We were getting along and…"

"It's evident you still have an issue with timing," Phoenix snapped.

Her comment stung. Carter took a deep breath and exhaled slowly. He tried not to lose his patience with her.

"I'm sorry. I shouldn't have said that." Phoenix carefully stepped over the threshold and turned back toward Carter.

"I'm sorry, too. Hopefully we can move on. It was nice being friendly. Maybe one day we could go back to that."

Phoenix looked away. When she looked back at Carter, there was something unreadable in her eyes. Had she been more affected by his news than he realized? Their eyes locked. Carter felt himself moving closer to her.

"We just need to get through the wedding tomorrow and the next few days, and we can go back to living our normal lives.

You won't have to see me and I won't have to see you."

Phoenix's words struck something in him. He didn't like the idea of never seeing her again. The past few days had awakened something in him. Even the tense moments reminded him of what he once loved about her. He remembered his own words… *The way I love you.*

Carter kept his eyes on hers. She held his gaze. Old feelings returned, stirring his emotions. Perhaps those feelings had never left and remained dormant in his soul. His heart quickened. Desire flooded him and he wondered what Phoenix would do if he kissed her. She still hadn't looked away. Was she waiting for him to leave? Did she want to kiss him as much as he wanted to kiss her? Maybe she was having some of the same wild thoughts. Maybe old feelings were coming to the surface for her, too.

Carter stepped closer to Phoenix. She didn't move. Carter noticed the rise and fall of her chest become more intense. He stepped closer. She stayed put. He watched her throat shift as she swallowed. He smelled the sweet scent of perfume. He wondered if he could taste the salt on her skin.

Carter wasn't sure if it was love, but he felt something. It was more than lust. He missed Phoenix. The thought of her absence burned in him. In this moment he realized every woman since her had been an attempted replacement. That's why none of those relationships worked. But Phoenix would never have him. Would she?

Don't miss what happens next in…
One More Second Chance *by Nicki Night.*

Available August 2021 wherever
Harlequin Desire books and ebooks are sold.

Harlequin.com